AMERICAN MIDNIGHT

AMERICAN MIDNIGHT

Tales of the Dark

SELECTED AND INTRODUCED
BY LAIRD HUNT

PUSHKIN PRESS
LONDON

Pushkin Press
71–75 Shelton Street
London WC2H 9JQ

First published by Pushkin Press in 2019

3 5 7 9 8 6 4 2

ISBN 13: 978-1-78227-595-4

Designed and typeset by Tetragon, London
Printed and bound in Great Britain by TJ Books Limited, Padstow, Cornwall on Munken Premium White 80gsm

www.pushkinpress.com

CONTENTS

INTRODUCTION

"Shiver by shiver, we gain insight."

Guillermo del Toro,
Foreword to *Haunted Castles: The Complete Gothic Stories of Ray Russell*

SOMEWHERE AROUND MIDNIGHT, when I was six or seven and staying with my family on my grandmother's Indiana farm, as I lay in a creaky bed in a small bedroom at the back of the old house, I saw the ghost of a baby floating above me. The baby was life-sized and dressed in a stiff white gown. It was glowing. And weeping. They were not tears of joy. I couldn't move. The wailing grew louder, almost siren-like, and this eventually released me. I sprang out of bed, threw off my covers. Howls were coming from the room down the hall where my younger cousin was staying. By and by, I could hear her parents telling her she'd had a nightmare and should go back to sleep. I went back to sleep too.

In the morning when I told my parents about the ghost, they said that clearly I'd heard my cousin, who was not much more than a baby herself, and so had dreamed up this visitor. I did not believe them. I said that the sad little ghost had been summoned by my cousin's crying, that it had slipped in under the cover of her tears. In an investigative spirit, I asked my grandmother if any babies had ever died on the farm. My grandmother said something to the effect that in fact she herself had been in that inconvenient condition on the farm when she was first born, and that if a doctor's assistant hadn't pumped icy water on her at the kitchen sink while the attending doctor took care of her mother, she would be in that inconvenient condition still. My parents—ever eager to rationalize and no doubt not yet far into their first cups of coffee—then said that probably I had already heard this story about my grandmother's still birth and revival without realizing it, and that my cousin's crying had helped craft the submerged memory into a nightmare.

"But I was awake the whole time! It was Grandma's ghost! She sounded angry!" I said.

"Grandma is right here," they said.

"But she died, she said so!" I said.

"Go out and play," they said.

And that is what I did.

The ghost didn't return that night or any other, but I remembered. So that when, many years later, I came across Edith Wharton's chilling 'The Eyes', a classic of a fireside frame story if ever there was one—"We had been put in the mood for ghosts, that evening, after an excellent dinner at our old friend Culwin's..."—I experienced the deep-night bedside appearance of the awful titular eyes as a disturbing echo. Wharton may well have meant to impart a moral lesson by positing their repeated appearance (Culwin is more than moderately a jerk), but to me they rhymed quite viscerally with my own earliest horror in the dark. A memory that to this day—along with the implication of my grandmother's remarks: that the baby ghost could very well have been her—gives me chills.

Scary stories bang at our deep bells, the ones that live in the pit of our stomachs, at the base of our spines. They take different shapes, do it in different ways. Indeed, each of the nine tales gathered here glitters with a particular malevolence all its own. Nathaniel Hawthorne's 'Young Goodman Brown', long a personal favourite, blends familiar tropes of the genre—distant past, dark night, deep woods—with the awful anxiety of uncertainty and the unmooring terrors, especially in a religious age, of wavering faith. Charlotte Perkins Gilman's 'The Yellow Wallpaper' centres on oppressive isolation and the slow but steady unmaking of a mind, while Zora Neale Hurston's 'Spunk', a tale of blatant guilt and gruesome comeuppance, is a reminder that if too often in real life Goliath clubs him down, ghostly David, armed with a sling of righteous spite, may yet come for him and take revenge. Edgar Allan Poe's 'The Masque of the Red Death', not the only one of these American tales to cast its gaze across the Atlantic, drops its hammer of judgement not on one or two people but on a thousand.

Poe was writing in 1842, but the apocalyptic premise continues to ring true (I for one now have Prince's '1999' in my head: "2000 zero zero party over oops out of time..."). I would wager that most reading this have been invited recently—whether in the pages of a book or on television or movie screens—to at least one haunting contemporary equivalent of Poe's "masked ball of the most unusual magnificence".

The other stories here, which range from frightening resurrections following scientific experiments gone hideously wrong to encounters with mournful ghosts holding vigil over the wrong bones, feel to me similarly fresh and frightening, as if they had been written not last night but no more than a few months ago. Recently, in fact, when I was rewatching Jordan Peele's extraordinary 2017 film *Get Out*, which folds layers of humour in with its horror, I thought of Mark Twain's 'A Ghost Story', which is scary, sad and very funny in turn.

I said at the start that Edith Wharton's ghostly eyes yanked me back to that creaking bed of my childhood, and so Emma Frances Dawson's weird and relatively little-known 'An Itinerant House' (recommended to me by the excellent writer of contemporary dark tales Brian Evenson) also brought back memories of that time. The story is set in a San Francisco that Ambrose Bierce, in discussing Dawson's work, characterized as "a city of wraiths and things forbidden to the senses". There are no bedside spectres here, but by exploring the activated agency of a person who is no longer dead, the tale reminded me of my grandmother's return from death. Unlike Felipa, my grandmother used her own early step back from the brink as motivation to build a long, good life as a Latin teacher and greenhouse-business owner, not to toss terrible curses, but the bell got rung for me nonetheless, and the ghost of a baby my grandmother either was or wasn't floated up once again.

While I certainly wouldn't wish a remembered apparition like that one on anybody, I do hope these stories, culled from a century of shiver-inducing American output, will work their magic on you as they have on me. And, just in case, if you read them at night, I'd suggest keeping the lights on for a while after you've put the book down.

LAIRD HUNT, 2019

THE MASQUE OF THE RED DEATH

Edgar Allan Poe

THE "RED DEATH" had long devastated the country. No pestilence had ever been so fatal, or so hideous. Blood was its Avatar and its seal—the redness and the horror of blood. There were sharp pains, and sudden dizziness, and then profuse bleeding at the pores, with dissolution. The scarlet stains upon the body and especially upon the face of the victim, were the pest ban which shut him out from the aid and from the sympathy of his fellow men. And the whole seizure, progress and termination of the disease, were the incidents of half an hour.

But the Prince Prospero was happy and dauntless and sagacious. When his dominions were half depopulated, he summoned to his presence a thousand hale and light-hearted friends from among the knights and dames of his court, and with these retired to the deep seclusion of one of his castellated abbeys. This was an extensive and magnificent structure, the creation of the prince's own eccentric yet august taste. A strong and lofty wall girdled it in. This wall had gates of iron. The courtiers, having entered, brought furnaces and massy hammers and welded the bolts. They resolved to leave means neither of ingress nor egress to the sudden impulses of despair or of frenzy from within. The abbey was amply provisioned. With such precautions the courtiers might bid defiance to contagion. The external world could take care of itself. In the meantime it was folly to grieve, or to think. The prince had provided all the appliances of pleasure. There were buffoons, there were improvisatori, there were ballet dancers, there were musicians, there was Beauty, there was wine. All these and security were within. Without was the "Red Death".

It was towards the close of the fifth or sixth month of his seclusion, and while the pestilence raged most furiously abroad, that the Prince Prospero entertained his thousand friends at a masked ball of the most unusual magnificence.

It was a voluptuous scene, that masquerade. But first let me tell of the rooms in which it was held.

These were seven—an imperial suite. In many palaces, however, such suites form a long and straight vista, while the folding doors slide back nearly to the walls on either hand, so that the view of the whole extent is scarcely impeded. Here the case was very different, as might have been expected from the duke's love of the *bizarre*. The apartments were so irregularly disposed that the vision embraced but little more than one at a time. There was a sharp turn at every twenty or thirty yards, and at each turn a novel effect. To the right and left, in the middle of each wall, a tall and narrow Gothic window looked out upon a closed corridor which pursued the windings of the suite. These windows were of stained glass whose colour varied in accordance with the prevailing hue of the decorations of the chamber into which it opened. That at the eastern extremity was hung, for example, in blue—and vividly blue were its windows. The second chamber was purple in its ornaments and tapestries, and here the panes were purple. The third was green throughout, and so were the casements. The fourth was furnished and lighted with orange—the fifth with white—the sixth with violet. The seventh apartment was closely shrouded in black velvet tapestries that hung all over the ceiling and down the walls, falling in heavy folds upon a carpet of the same material and hue. But in this chamber only, the colour of the windows failed to correspond with the decorations. The panes here were scarlet—a deep blood colour. Now in no one of the seven apartments was there any lamp or candelabrum, amid the profusion of golden ornaments that lay scattered to and fro or depended from the roof. There was no light of any kind emanating from lamp or candle within the suite of chambers. But in the corridors that followed the suite, there stood, opposite to each window, a heavy tripod, bearing a brazier of fire, that projected its rays through the tinted glass and so glaringly illumined the room. And thus were produced a multitude of gaudy and fantastic appearances. But in the western or black chamber the effect of the firelight that streamed upon the dark hangings through the blood-tinted panes, was ghastly in the extreme, and produced so wild a look upon the countenances of those who entered, that there were few of the company bold enough to set foot within its precincts at all.

It was in this apartment, also, that there stood against the western wall, a gigantic clock of ebony. Its pendulum swung to and fro with a dull, heavy, monotonous clang; and when the minute hand made the circuit of the face, and the hour was to be stricken, there came from the brazen lungs of the clock a sound which was clear and loud and deep and exceedingly musical, but of so peculiar a note and emphasis that, at each lapse of an hour, the musicians of the orchestra were constrained to pause, momentarily, in their performance, to harken to the sound; and thus the waltzers perforce ceased their evolutions; and there was a brief disconcert of the whole gay company; and, while the chimes of the clock yet rang, it was observed that the giddiest grew pale, and the more aged and sedate passed their hands over their brows as if in confused reverie or meditation. But when the echoes had fully ceased, a light laughter at once pervaded the assembly; the musicians looked at each other and smiled as if at their own nervousness and folly, and made whispering vows, each to the other, that the next chiming of the clock should produce in them no similar emotion; and then, after the lapse of sixty minutes (which embrace three thousand and six hundred seconds of the Time that flies), there came yet another chiming of the clock, and then were the same disconcert and tremulousness and meditation as before.

But, in spite of these things, it was a gay and magnificent revel. The tastes of the duke were peculiar. He had a fine eye for colours and effects. He disregarded the *decora* of mere fashion. His plans were bold and fiery, and his conceptions glowed with barbaric lustre. There are some who would have thought him mad. His followers felt that he was not. It was necessary to hear and see and touch him to be *sure* that he was not.

He had directed, in great part, the movable embellishments of the seven chambers, upon occasion of this great *fête*; and it was his own guiding taste which had given character to the masqueraders. Be sure they were grotesque. There were much glare and glitter and piquancy and phantasm—much of what has been since seen in *Hernani*. There were arabesque figures with unsuited limbs and appointments. There were delirious fancies such as the madman fashions. There were much of the beautiful, much of the wanton, much of the bizarre, something of the terrible, and not a little of that which might have excited disgust. To and fro in the seven chambers there stalked, in fact, a multitude of dreams. And these—the dreams—writhed in and about taking hue from the rooms, and causing the wild music of the orchestra to seem as the echo of their steps. And, anon, there strikes the ebony clock which stands in the hall of the velvet. And then, for a moment, all is still, and all is silent save the voice of the clock. The dreams are stiff-frozen as they stand. But the echoes of the chime die away—they have endured but an instant—and a light, half-subdued laughter floats after them as they depart. And now again the music swells, and the dreams live, and writhe to and fro more merrily than ever, taking hue from the many tinted windows through which stream the rays from the tripods. But to the chamber which lies most westwardly of the seven, there are now none of the maskers who venture; for the night is waning away; and there flows a ruddier light through the blood-coloured panes; and the blackness of the sable drapery appals; and to him whose foot falls upon the sable carpet, there comes from the near clock of ebony a muffled peal more solemnly emphatic than any which reaches *their* ears who indulged in the more remote gaieties of the other apartments.

But these other apartments were densely crowded, and in them beat feverishly the heart of life. And the revel went whirlingly on, until at length there commenced the sounding of midnight upon the clock.

And then the music ceased, as I have told; and the evolutions of the waltzers were quieted; and there was an uneasy cessation of all things as before. But now there were twelve strokes to be sounded by the bell of the clock; and thus it happened, perhaps, that more of thought crept, with more of time, into the meditations of the thoughtful among those who revelled. And thus too, it happened, perhaps, that before the last echoes of the last chime had utterly sunk into silence, there were many individuals in the crowd who had found leisure to become aware of the presence of a masked figure which had arrested the attention of no single individual before. And the rumour of this new presence having spread itself whisperingly around, there arose at length from the whole company a buzz, or murmur, expressive of disapprobation and surprise—then, finally, of terror, of horror, and of disgust.

In an assembly of phantasms such as I have painted, it may well be supposed that no ordinary appearance could have excited such sensation. In truth the masquerade licence of the night was nearly unlimited; but the figure in question had out-Heroded Herod, and gone beyond the bounds of even the prince's indefinite decorum. There are chords in the hearts of the most reckless which cannot be touched without emotion. Even with the utterly lost, to whom life and death are equally jests, there are matters of which no jest can be made. The whole company, indeed, seemed now deeply to feel that in the costume and bearing of the stranger neither wit nor propriety existed. The figure was tall and gaunt, and shrouded from head to foot in the habiliments of the grave. The mask which concealed the visage was made so nearly to resemble the countenance of a stiffened corpse that the closest scrutiny must have had difficulty in detecting the cheat. And yet all this might have been endured, if not approved, by the mad revellers around. But the mummer had gone so far as to assume the type of the Red Death. His vesture was dabbled in *blood*—and his broad brow, with all the features of the face, was besprinkled with the scarlet horror.

When the eyes of the Prince Prospero fell upon this spectral image (which, with a slow and solemn movement, as if more fully to sustain its role, stalked to and fro among the waltzers) he was seen to be convulsed, in the first moment with a strong shudder either of terror or distaste; but, in the next, his brow reddened with rage.

"Who dares,"—he demanded hoarsely of the courtiers who stood near him—"who dares insult us with this blasphemous mockery? Seize him and unmask him—that we may know whom we have to hang, at sunrise, from the battlements!"

It was in the eastern or blue chamber in which stood the Prince Prospero as he uttered these words. They rang throughout the seven rooms loudly and clearly, for the prince was a bold and robust man, and the music had become hushed at the waving of his hand.

It was in the blue room where stood the prince, with a group of pale courtiers by his side. At first, as he spoke, there was a slight rushing movement of this group in the direction of the intruder, who at the moment was also near at hand, and now, with deliberate and stately step, made closer approach to the speaker. But from a certain nameless awe with which the mad assumptions of the mummer had inspired the whole party, there were found none who put forth hand to seize him; so that, unimpeded, he passed within a yard of the prince's person; and, while the vast assembly, as if with one impulse, shrank from the centres of the rooms to the walls, he made his way uninterruptedly, but with the same solemn and measured step which had distinguished him from the first, through the blue chamber to the purple—through the purple to the green—through the green to the orange—through this again to the white—and even thence to the violet, ere a decided movement had been made to arrest him. It was then, however, that the Prince Prospero, maddening with rage and the shame of his own momentary cowardice, rushed hurriedly through the six chambers, while none followed him on account of a deadly terror that had seized upon all. He bore aloft a drawn dagger, and had approached, in rapid impetuosity, to within three or four feet of the retreating figure, when the latter, having attained the extremity of the velvet apartment, turned suddenly and confronted his pursuer. There was a sharp cry—and the dagger dropped gleaming upon the sable carpet, upon which, instantly afterwards, fell prostrate in death the Prince Prospero. Then, summoning the wild courage of despair, a throng of the revellers at once threw themselves into the black apartment, and, seizing the mummer, whose tall figure stood erect and motionless within the shadow of the ebony clock, gasped in unutterable horror at finding the grave cerements and corpse-like mask, which they handled with so violent a rudeness, untenanted by any tangible form.

And now was acknowledged the presence of the Red Death. He had come like a thief in the night. And one by one dropped the revellers in the blood-bedewed halls of their revel, and died each in the despairing posture of his fall. And the life of the ebony clock went out with that of the last of the gay. And the flames of the tripods expired. And Darkness and Decay and the Red Death held illimitable dominion over all.

YOUNG GOODMAN BROWN

Nathaniel Hawthorne

YOUNG GOODMAN BROWN came forth at sunset into the street at Salem village; but put his head back, after crossing the threshold, to exchange a parting kiss with his young wife. And Faith, as the wife was aptly named, thrust her own pretty head into the street, letting the wind play with the pink ribbons of her cap while she called to Goodman Brown.

"Dearest heart," whispered she, softly and rather sadly, when her lips were close to his ear, "prithee put off your journey until sunrise and sleep in your own bed tonight. A lone woman is troubled with such dreams and such thoughts that she's afeard of herself sometimes. Pray tarry with me this night, dear husband, of all nights in the year."

"My love and my Faith," replied young Goodman Brown, "of all nights in the year, this one night must

I tarry away from thee. My journey, as thou callest it, forth and back again, must needs be done 'twixt now and sunrise. What, my sweet, pretty wife, dost thou doubt me already, and we but three months married?"

"Then God bless you!" said Faith, with the pink ribbons; "and may you find all well when you come back."

"Amen!" cried Goodman Brown. "Say thy prayers, dear Faith, and go to bed at dusk, and no harm will come to thee."

So they parted; and the young man pursued his way until, being about to turn the corner by the meeting house, he looked back and saw the head of Faith still peeping after him with a melancholy air, in spite of her pink ribbons.

"Poor little Faith!" thought he, for his heart smote him. "What a wretch am I to leave her on such an errand! She talks of dreams, too. Methought as she spoke there was trouble in her face, as if a dream had warned her what work is to be done tonight. But no, no; 'twould kill her to think it. Well, she's a blessed angel on earth; and after this one night I'll cling to her skirts and follow her to heaven."

With this excellent resolve for the future, Goodman Brown felt himself justified in making more haste on his present evil purpose. He had taken a dreary road, darkened by all the gloomiest trees of the forest, which barely stood aside to let the narrow path creep through, and closed immediately behind. It was all as lonely as could be; and there is this peculiarity in such a solitude, that the traveller knows not who may be concealed by the innumerable trunks and the thick boughs overhead; so that with lonely footsteps he may yet be passing through an unseen multitude.

"There may be a devilish Indian behind every tree," said Goodman Brown to himself; and he glanced fearfully behind him as he added, "What if the devil himself should be at my very elbow!"

His head being turned back, he passed a crook of the road, and, looking forward again, beheld the figure of a man, in grave and decent attire, seated at the foot of an old tree. He arose at Goodman Brown's approach and walked onward side by side with him.

"You are late, Goodman Brown," said he. "The clock of the Old South was striking as I came through Boston, and that is full fifteen minutes agone."

"Faith kept me back a while," replied the young man, with a tremor in his voice, caused by the sudden appearance of his companion, though not wholly unexpected.

It was now deep dusk in the forest, and deepest in that part of it where these two were journeying. As nearly as could be discerned, the second traveller was about fifty years old, apparently in the same rank of life as Goodman Brown, and bearing a considerable resemblance to him, though perhaps more in expression than features. Still they might have been taken for father and son. And yet, though the elder person was as simply clad as the younger, and as simple in manner too, he had an indescribable air of one who knew the world, and who would not have felt abashed at the governor's dinner table or in King William's court, were it possible that his affairs should call him thither. But the only thing about him that could be fixed upon as remarkable was his staff, which bore the likeness of a great black snake, so curiously wrought that it might almost be seen to twist and wriggle itself like a living serpent. This, of course, must have been an ocular deception, assisted by the uncertain light.

"Come, Goodman Brown," cried his fellow traveller, "this is a dull pace for the beginning of a journey. Take my staff, if you are so soon weary."

"Friend," said the other, exchanging his slow pace for a full stop, "having kept covenant by meeting thee here, it is my purpose now to return whence I came. I have scruples touching the matter thou wot'st of."

"Sayest thou so?" replied he of the serpent, smiling apart. "Let us walk on, nevertheless, reasoning as we go; and if I convince thee not thou shalt turn back. We are but a little way in the forest yet."

"Too far! too far!" exclaimed the goodman, unconsciously resuming his walk. "My father never went into the woods on such an errand, nor his father before him. We have been a race of honest men and good Christians since the days of the martyrs; and shall I be the first of the name of Brown that ever took this path and kept—"

"Such company, thou wouldst say," observed the elder person, interpreting his pause. "Well said, Goodman Brown! I have been as well acquainted with your family as with ever a one among the Puritans; and that's no trifle to say. I helped your grandfather, the constable, when he lashed the Quaker woman so smartly through the streets of Salem; and it was I that brought your father a pitch-pine knot, kindled at my own hearth, to set fire to an Indian village, in King Philip's war. They were my good friends, both; and many a pleasant walk have we had along this path, and returned merrily after midnight. I would fain be friends with you for their sake."

"If it be as thou sayest," replied Goodman Brown, "I marvel they never spoke of these matters; or, verily, I marvel not, seeing that the least rumor of the sort would have driven them from New England. We are a people of prayer, and good works to boot, and abide no such wickedness."

"Wickedness or not," said the traveller with the twisted staff, "I have a very general acquaintance here in New England. The deacons of many a church have drunk the communion wine with me; the selectmen of divers towns make me their chairman; and a majority of the Great and General Court are firm supporters of my interest. The governor and I, too— But these are state secrets."

"Can this be so?" cried Goodman Brown, with a stare of amazement at his undisturbed companion. "Howbeit, I have nothing to do with the governor and council; they have their own ways, and are no rule for a simple husbandman like me. But, were I to go on with thee, how should I meet the eye of that good old man, our minister, at Salem village? Oh, his voice would make me tremble both Sabbath day and lecture day."

Thus far the elder traveller had listened with due gravity; but now burst into a fit of irrepressible mirth, shaking himself so violently that his snake-like staff actually seemed to wriggle in sympathy.

"Ha! ha! ha!" shouted he again and again; then composing himself, "Well, go on, Goodman Brown, go on; but, prithee, don't kill me with laughing."

"Well, then, to end the matter at once," said Goodman Brown, considerably nettled, "there is my wife, Faith. It would break her dear little heart; and I'd rather break my own."

"Nay, if that be the case," answered the other, "e'en go thy ways, Goodman Brown. I would not for twenty old women like the one hobbling before us that Faith should come to any harm."

As he spoke he pointed his staff at a female figure on the path, in whom Goodman Brown recognized a very pious and exemplary dame, who had taught him his catechism in youth, and was still his moral and spiritual adviser, jointly with the minister and Deacon Gookin.

"A marvel, truly, that Goody Cloyse should be so far in the wilderness at nightfall," said he. "But with your leave, friend, I shall take a cut through the woods until we have left this Christian woman behind. Being a stranger to you, she might ask whom I was consorting with and whither I was going."

"Be it so," said his fellow traveller. "Betake you to the woods, and let me keep the path."

Accordingly the young man turned aside, but took care to watch his companion, who advanced softly along the road until he had come within a staff's length of the old dame. She, meanwhile, was making the best of her way, with singular speed for so aged a woman, and mumbling some indistinct words—a prayer, doubtless—as she went. The traveller put forth his staff and touched her withered neck with what seemed the serpent's tail.

"The devil!" screamed the pious old lady.

"Then Goody Cloyse knows her old friend?" observed the traveller, confronting her and leaning on his writhing stick.

"Ah, forsooth, and is it your worship indeed?" cried the good dame. "Yea, truly is it, and in the very image of my old gossip, Goodman Brown, the grandfather of the silly fellow that now is. But—would your worship believe it?—my broomstick hath strangely disappeared, stolen, as I suspect, by that unhanged witch, Goody Cory, and that, too, when I was all anointed with the juice of smallage, and cinquefoil, and wolf's bane."

"Mingled with fine wheat and the fat of a new-born babe," said the shape of old Goodman Brown.

"Ah, your worship knows the recipe," cried the old lady, cackling aloud. "So, as I was saying, being all ready for the meeting, and no horse to ride on, I made up my mind to foot it; for they tell me there is a nice young man to be taken into communion tonight. But now your good worship will lend me your arm, and we shall be there in a twinkling."

"That can hardly be," answered her friend. "I may not spare you my arm, Goody Cloyse; but here is my staff, if you will."

So saying, he threw it down at her feet, where, perhaps, it assumed life, being one of the rods which its owner had formerly lent to the Egyptian magi. Of this fact, however, Goodman Brown could not take cognizance. He had cast up his eyes in astonishment, and, looking down again, beheld neither Goody Cloyse nor the serpentine staff, but his fellow traveller alone, who waited for him as calmly as if nothing had happened.

"That old woman taught me my catechism," said the young man; and there was a world of meaning in this simple comment.

They continued to walk onward, while the elder

traveller exhorted his companion to make good speed and persevere in the path, discoursing so aptly that his arguments seemed rather to spring up in the bosom of his auditor than to be suggested by himself. As they went, he plucked a branch of maple to serve for a walking stick, and began to strip it of the twigs and little boughs, which were wet with evening dew. The moment his fingers touched them they became strangely withered and dried up as with a week's sunshine. Thus the pair proceeded, at a good free pace, until suddenly, in a gloomy hollow of the road, Goodman Brown sat himself down on the stump of a tree and refused to go any farther.

"Friend," said he, stubbornly, "my mind is made up. Not another step will I budge on this errand. What if a wretched old woman do choose to go to the devil when I thought she was going to heaven: is that any reason why I should quit my dear Faith and go after her?"

"You will think better of this by and by," said his acquaintance, composedly. "Sit here and rest yourself awhile; and when you feel like moving again, there is my staff to help you along."

Without more words, he threw his companion the maple stick, and was as speedily out of sight as if he had vanished into the deepening gloom. The young man sat a few moments by the roadside, applauding himself greatly, and thinking with how clear a conscience he should meet the minister in his morning walk, nor shrink from the eye of good old Deacon Gookin. And what calm sleep would be his that very night, which was to have been spent so wickedly, but so purely and sweetly now, in the arms of Faith! Amidst these pleasant and praiseworthy meditations, Goodman Brown heard the tramp of horses along the road, and deemed it advisable to conceal himself within the verge of the forest, conscious of the guilty purpose that had brought him thither, though now so happily turned from it.

On came the hoof tramps and the voices of the riders, two grave old voices, conversing soberly as they drew near. These mingled sounds appeared to pass along the road, within a few yards of the young man's hiding place; but, owing doubtless to the depth of the gloom at that particular spot, neither the travellers nor their steeds were visible. Though their figures brushed the small boughs by the wayside, it could not be seen that they intercepted, even for a moment, the faint gleam from the strip of bright sky athwart which they must have passed. Goodman

Brown alternately crouched and stood on tiptoe, pulling aside the branches and thrusting forth his head as far as he durst without discerning so much as a shadow. It vexed him the more, because he could have sworn, were such a thing possible, that he recognized the voices of the minister and Deacon Gookin, jogging along quietly, as they were wont to do, when bound to some ordination or ecclesiastical council. While yet within hearing, one of the riders stopped to pluck a switch.

"Of the two, reverend sir," said the voice like the deacon's, "I had rather miss an ordination dinner than tonight's meeting. They tell me that some of our community are to be here from Falmouth and beyond, and others from Connecticut and Rhode Island, besides several of the Indian powwows, who, after their fashion, know almost as much deviltry as the best of us. Moreover, there is a goodly young woman to be taken into communion."

"Mighty well, Deacon Gookin!" replied the solemn old tones of the minister. "Spur up, or we shall be late. Nothing can be done, you know, until I get on the ground."

The hoofs clattered again; and the voices, talking so strangely in the empty air, passed on through the forest, where no church had ever been gathered or solitary Christian prayed. Whither, then, could these holy men be journeying so deep into the heathen wilderness? Young Goodman Brown caught hold of a tree for support, being ready to sink down on the ground, faint and overburdened with the heavy sickness of his heart. He looked up to the sky, doubting whether there really was a heaven above him. Yet there was the blue arch, and the stars brightening in it.

"With heaven above and Faith below, I will yet stand firm against the devil!" cried Goodman Brown.

While he still gazed upward into the deep arch of the firmament and had lifted his hands to pray, a cloud, though no wind was stirring, hurried across the zenith and hid the brightening stars. The blue sky was still visible, except directly overhead, where this black mass of cloud was sweeping swiftly northward. Aloft in the air, as if from the depths of the cloud, came a confused and doubtful sound of voices. Once the listener fancied that he could distinguish the accents of townspeople of his own, men and women, both pious and ungodly, many of whom he had met at the communion table, and had seen others rioting at the tavern. The next moment, so indistinct were the sounds, he doubted whether he had heard aught but the murmur of the old forest, whispering without a wind. Then came a stronger swell of those familiar tones, heard daily in the sunshine at Salem village, but never until now from a cloud of night. There was one voice of a young woman, uttering lamentations, yet with an uncertain sorrow, and entreating for some favor, which, perhaps, it would grieve her to obtain; and all the unseen multitude, both saints and sinners, seemed to encourage her onward.

"Faith!" shouted Goodman Brown, in a voice of agony and desperation; and the echoes of the forest mocked him, crying, "Faith! Faith!" as if bewildered wretches were seeking her all through the wilderness.

The cry of grief, rage, and terror was yet piercing the night, when the unhappy husband held his breath for a response. There was a scream, drowned immediately in a louder murmur of voices, fading into far-off laughter, as the dark cloud swept away, leaving the clear and silent sky above Goodman Brown. But something fluttered lightly down through the air and caught on the branch of a tree. The young man seized it, and beheld a pink ribbon.

"My Faith is gone!" cried he, after one stupefied moment. "There is no good on earth; and sin is but a name. Come, devil; for to thee is this world given."

And, maddened with despair, so that he laughed loud and long, did Goodman Brown grasp his staff and set forth again, at such a rate that he seemed to fly along the forest path rather than to walk or run. The road grew wilder and drearier and more faintly traced, and vanished at length, leaving him in the heart of the dark wilderness, still rushing onward with the instinct that guides mortal man to evil. The whole forest was peopled with frightful sounds—the creaking of the trees, the howling of wild beasts, and the yell of Indians; while sometimes the wind tolled like a distant church bell, and sometimes gave a broad roar around the traveller, as if all Nature were laughing him to scorn. But he was himself the chief horror of the scene, and shrank not from its other horrors.

"Ha! ha! ha!" roared Goodman Brown when the wind laughed at him.

"Let us hear which will laugh loudest. Think not to frighten me with your deviltry. Come witch, come wizard, come Indian powwow, come devil himself, and here comes Goodman Brown. You may as well fear him as he fear you."

In truth, all through the haunted forest there could be nothing more frightful than the figure of

Goodman Brown. On he flew among the black pines, brandishing his staff with frenzied gestures, now giving vent to an inspiration of horrid blasphemy, and now shouting forth such laughter as set all the echoes of the forest laughing like demons around him. The fiend in his own shape is less hideous than when he rages in the breast of man. Thus sped the demoniac on his course, until, quivering among the trees, he saw a red light before him, as when the felled trunks and branches of a clearing have been set on fire, and throw up their lurid blaze against the sky, at the hour of midnight. He paused, in a lull of the tempest that had driven him onward, and heard the swell of what seemed a hymn, rolling solemnly from a distance with the weight of many voices. He knew the tune; it was a familiar one in the choir of the village meeting house. The verse died heavily away, and was lengthened by a chorus, not of human voices, but of all the sounds of the benighted wilderness pealing in awful harmony together. Goodman Brown cried out, and his cry was lost to his own ear by its unison with the cry of the desert.

In the interval of silence he stole forward until the light glared full upon his eyes. At one extremity of an open space, hemmed in by the dark wall of the forest, arose a rock, bearing some rude, natural resemblance either to an altar or a pulpit, and surrounded by four blazing pines, their tops aflame, their stems untouched, like candles at an evening meeting. The mass of foliage that had overgrown the summit of the rock was all on fire, blazing high into the night and fitfully illuminating the whole field. Each pendent twig and leafy festoon was in a blaze. As the red light arose and fell, a numerous congregation alternately shone forth, then disappeared in shadow, and again grew, as it were, out of the darkness, peopling the heart of the solitary woods at once.

"A grave and dark-clad company," quoth Goodman Brown.

In truth they were such. Among them, quivering to and fro between gloom and splendor, appeared faces that would be seen next day at the council board of the province, and others which, Sabbath after Sabbath, looked devoutly heavenward, and benignantly over the crowded pews, from the holiest pulpits in the land. Some affirm that the lady of the governor was there. At least there were high dames well known to her, and wives of honored husbands, and widows, a great multitude, and ancient maidens, all of excellent repute, and fair young girls, who trembled lest their mothers should espy them. Either the sudden gleams of light flashing over the obscure field bedazzled Goodman Brown, or he recognized a score of the church members of Salem village famous for their especial sanctity. Good old Deacon Gookin had arrived, and waited at the skirts of that venerable saint, his revered pastor. But, irreverently consorting with these grave, reputable, and pious people, these elders of the church, these chaste dames and dewy virgins, there were men of dissolute lives and women of spotted fame, wretches given over to all mean and filthy vice, and suspected even of horrid crimes. It was strange to see that the good shrank not from the wicked, nor were the sinners abashed by the saints. Scattered also among their pale-faced enemies were the Indian priests, or powwows, who had often scared their native forest with more hideous incantations than any known to English witchcraft.

"But where is Faith?" thought Goodman Brown; and, as hope came into his heart, he trembled.

Another verse of the hymn arose, a slow and mournful strain, such as the pious love, but joined to words which expressed all that our nature can conceive of sin, and darkly hinted at far more. Unfathomable to mere mortals is the lore of fiends.

Verse after verse was sung; and still the chorus of the desert swelled between like the deepest tone of a mighty organ; and with the final peal of that dreadful anthem there came a sound, as if the roaring wind, the rushing streams, the howling beasts, and every other voice of the unconcerted wilderness were mingling and according with the voice of guilty man in homage to the prince of all. The four blazing pines threw up a loftier flame, and obscurely discovered shapes and visages of horror on the smoke wreaths above the impious assembly. At the same moment the fire on the rock shot redly forth and formed a glowing arch above its base, where now appeared a figure. With reverence be it spoken, the figure bore no slight similitude, both in garb and manner, to some grave divine of the New England churches.

"Bring forth the converts!" cried a voice that echoed through the field and rolled into the forest.

At the word, Goodman Brown stepped forth from the shadow of the trees and approached the congregation, with whom he felt a loathful brotherhood by the sympathy of all that was wicked in his heart. He could have well-nigh sworn that the shape of his own dead father beckoned him to advance, looking downward from a smoke wreath, while a woman, with dim features of despair, threw out her hand to warn him back. Was it his mother? But he had no power to retreat one step, nor to resist, even in thought, when the minister and good old Deacon Gookin seized his arms and led him to the blazing rock. Thither came also the slender form of a veiled female, led between Goody Cloyse, that pious teacher of the catechism, and Martha Carrier, who had received the devil's promise to be queen of hell. A rampant hag was she. And there stood the proselytes beneath the canopy of fire.

"Welcome, my children," said the dark figure, "to the communion of your race. Ye have found thus young your nature and your destiny. My children, look behind you!"

They turned; and flashing forth, as it were, in a sheet of flame, the fiend worshippers were seen; the smile of welcome gleamed darkly on every visage.

"There," resumed the sable form, "are all whom ye have reverenced from youth. Ye deemed them holier than yourselves, and shrank from your own sin, contrasting it with their lives of righteousness and prayerful aspirations heavenward. Yet here are they all in my worshipping assembly. This night it shall be granted you to know their secret deeds: how hoary-bearded elders of the church have whispered wanton words to the young maids of their households; how many a woman, eager for widows' weeds, has given her husband a drink at bedtime and let him sleep his last sleep in her bosom; how beardless youths have made haste to inherit their fathers' wealth; and how fair damsels—blush not, sweet ones—have dug little graves in the garden, and bidden me, the sole guest to an infant's funeral. By the sympathy of your human hearts for sin ye shall scent out all the places—whether in church, bedchamber, street, field, or forest—where crime has been committed, and shall exult to behold the whole earth one stain of guilt, one mighty blood spot. Far more than this. It shall be yours to penetrate, in every bosom, the deep mystery of sin, the fountain of all wicked arts, and which inexhaustibly supplies more evil impulses than human power—than my power at its utmost—can make manifest in deeds. And now, my children, look upon each other."

They did so; and, by the blaze of the hell-kindled torches, the wretched man beheld his Faith, and the wife her husband, trembling before that unhallowed altar.

"Lo, there ye stand, my children," said the figure, in a deep and solemn tone, almost sad with its despairing awfulness, as if his once angelic nature could yet mourn for our miserable race. "Depending upon one another's hearts, ye had still hoped that virtue were not all a dream. Now are ye undeceived. Evil is the nature of mankind. Evil must be your only happiness. Welcome again, my children, to the communion of your race."

"Welcome," repeated the fiend worshippers, in one cry of despair and triumph.

And there they stood, the only pair, as it seemed, who were yet hesitating on the verge of wickedness in this dark world. A basin was hollowed, naturally, in the rock. Did it contain water, reddened by the lurid light? or was it blood? or, perchance, a liquid flame? Herein did the shape of evil dip his hand and prepare to lay the mark of baptism upon their foreheads, that they might be partakers of the mystery of sin, more conscious of the secret guilt of others, both in deed and thought, than they could now be of their own. The husband cast one look at his pale wife, and Faith at him. What polluted wretches would the next glance show them to each other, shuddering alike at what they disclosed and what they saw!

"Faith! Faith!" cried the husband, "look up to heaven, and resist the wicked one."

Whether Faith obeyed he knew not. Hardly had he spoken when he found himself amid calm night and solitude, listening to a roar of the wind which died heavily away through the forest. He staggered against the rock, and felt it chill and damp; while a hanging twig, that had been all on fire, besprinkled his cheek with the coldest dew.

The next morning young Goodman Brown came slowly into the street of Salem village, staring around him like a bewildered man. The good old minister was taking a walk along the graveyard to get an appetite for breakfast and meditate his sermon, and bestowed a blessing, as he passed, on Goodman Brown. He shrank from the venerable saint as if to avoid an anathema. Old Deacon Gookin was at domestic worship, and the holy words of his prayer were heard through the open window. "What God doth the wizard pray to?" quoth Goodman Brown. Goody Cloyse, that excellent old Christian, stood in the early sunshine at her own lattice, catechizing a little girl who had brought her a pint of morning's milk. Goodman Brown snatched away the child as from the grasp of the fiend himself. Turning the corner by the meeting house, he spied the head of Faith, with the pink ribbons, gazing anxiously forth, and bursting into such joy at sight of him that she skipped along the street and almost kissed her husband before the whole village. But Goodman Brown looked sternly and sadly into her face, and passed on without a greeting.

Had Goodman Brown fallen asleep in the forest and only dreamed a wild dream of a witch-meeting?

Be it so if you will; but, alas! it was a dream of evil omen for young Goodman Brown. A stern, a sad, a darkly meditative, a distrustful, if not a desperate man did he become from the night of that fearful dream. On the Sabbath day, when the congregation were singing a holy psalm, he could not listen because an anthem of sin rushed loudly upon his ear and drowned all the blessed strain. When the minister spoke from the pulpit with power and fervid eloquence, and, with his hand on the open Bible, of the sacred truths of our religion, and of saint-like lives and triumphant deaths, and of future bliss or misery unutterable, then did Goodman Brown turn pale, dreading lest the roof should thunder down upon the gray blasphemer and his hearers. Often, waking suddenly at midnight, he shrank from the bosom of Faith; and at morning or eventide, when the family knelt down at prayer, he scowled and muttered to himself, and gazed sternly at his wife, and turned away. And when he had lived long, and was borne to his grave a hoary corpse, followed by Faith, an aged woman, and children and grandchildren, a goodly procession, besides neighbors not a few, they carved no hopeful verse upon his tombstone, for his dying hour was gloom.

THE EYES

Edith Wharton

I

WE HAD BEEN put in the mood for ghosts, that evening, after an excellent dinner at our old friend Culwin's, by a tale of Fred Murchard's—the narrative of a strange personal visitation.

Seen through the haze of our cigars, and by the drowsy gleam of a coal fire, Culwin's library, with its oak walls and dark old bindings, made a good setting for such evocations; and ghostly experiences at first hand being, after Murchard's brilliant opening, the only kind acceptable to us, we proceeded to take stock of our group and tax each member for a contribution. There were eight of us, and seven contrived, in a manner more or less adequate, to fulfil the condition imposed. It surprised us all to find that we could muster such a show of supernatural impressions, for none of us, excepting Murchard himself and young Phil Frenham—whose story was the slightest of the lot—had the habit of sending our souls into the invisible. So that, on the whole, we had every reason to be proud of our seven "exhibits," and none of us would have dreamed of expecting an eighth from our host.

Our old friend, Mr. Andrew Culwin, who had sat back in his armchair, listening and blinking through the smoke circles with the cheerful tolerance of a wise old idol, was not the kind of man likely to be favoured with such contacts, though he had imagination enough to enjoy, without envying, the superior privileges of his guests. By age and by education he belonged to the stout Positivist tradition, and his habit of thought had been formed in the days of the epic struggle between physics and metaphysics. But he had been, then and always, essentially a spectator, a humorous detached observer of the immense muddled variety show of life, slipping out of his seat now and then for a brief dip into the convivialities at the back of the house, but never, as far as one knew, showing the least desire to jump on the stage and do a "turn."

Among his contemporaries there lingered a vague tradition of his having, at a remote period, and in a romantic clime, been wounded in a duel; but this legend no more tallied with what we younger men knew of his character than my mother's assertion that he had once been "a charming little man with nice eyes" corresponded to any possible reconstitution of his dry thwarted physiognomy.

"He never can have looked like anything but a bundle of sticks," Murchard had once said of him. "Or a phosphorescent log, rather," someone else amended; and we recognized the happiness of this description of his small squat trunk, with the red blink of the eyes in a face like mottled bark. He had always been possessed of a leisure which he had nursed and protected, instead of squandering it in vain activities. His carefully guarded hours had been devoted to the cultivation of a fine intelligence and a few judiciously chosen habits; and none of the disturbances common to human experience seemed to have crossed his sky. Nevertheless, his dispassionate survey of the universe had not raised his opinion of that costly experiment, and his study of the human race seemed to have resulted in the conclusion that all men were superfluous, and women necessary only because someone had to do the cooking. On the importance of this point his convictions were absolute, and gastronomy was the only science which he revered as dogma. It must be owned that his little dinners were a strong argument in favour of this view, besides being a reason—though not the main one—for the fidelity of his friends.

Mentally he exercised a hospitality less seductive but no less stimulating. His mind was like a forum, or some open meeting place for the exchange of ideas: somewhat cold and draughty, but light, spacious and orderly—a kind of academic grove from which all the leaves had fallen. In this privileged area a dozen of us were wont to stretch our muscles and expand our lungs; and, as if to prolong as much as possible the tradition of what we felt to be a vanishing institution, one or two neophytes were now and then added to our band.

Young Phil Frenham was the last, and the most interesting, of these recruits, and a good example of Murchard's somewhat morbid assertion that our old friend "liked 'em juicy." It was indeed a fact that Culwin, for all his mental dryness, specially tasted the lyric qualities in youth. As he was far too good an Epicurean to nip the flowers of soul which he gathered for his garden, his friendship was not a disintegrating influence: on the contrary, it forced the young idea to robuster bloom. And in Phil Frenham he had a fine subject for experimentation. The boy was really intelligent, and the soundness of his nature was like the pure paste under a delicate glaze. Culwin had fished him out of a thick fog of family dulness, and pulled him up to a peak in Darien; and the adventure hadn't hurt him a bit. Indeed, the skill with which Culwin had contrived to stimulate his curiosities without robbing them of their young bloom of awe seemed to me a sufficient answer to Murchard's ogreish metaphor. There was nothing hectic in Frenham's efflorescence, and his old friend had not laid even a fingertip on the sacred stupidities. One wanted no better proof of that than the fact that Frenham still reverenced them in Culwin.

"There's a side of him you fellows don't see. *I* believe that story about the duel!" he declared; and it was of the very essence of this belief that it should impel him—just as our little party was dispersing—to turn back to our host with the absurd demand: "And now you've got to tell us about *your* ghost!"

The outer door had closed on Murchard and the others; only Frenham and I remained; and the vigilant servant who presided over Culwin's destinies, having brought a fresh supply of soda-water, had been laconically ordered to bed.

Culwin's sociability was a night-blooming flower, and we knew that he expected the nucleus of his group to tighten around him after midnight. But Frenham's appeal seemed to disconcert him comically, and he rose from the chair in which he had just reseated himself after his farewells in the hall.

"*My* ghost? Do you suppose I'm fool enough to go to the expense of keeping one of my own, when there are so many charming ones in my friends' closets?—Take another cigar," he said, revolving toward me with a laugh.

Frenham laughed too, pulling up his slender height before the chimney piece as he turned to face his short bristling friend.

"Oh," he said, "you'd never be content to share if you met one you really liked."

Culwin had dropped back into his armchair, his shock head embedded in its habitual hollow, his little eyes glimmering over a fresh cigar.

"Liked—*liked*? Good Lord!" he growled.

"Ah, you *have*, then!" Frenham pounced on him in the same instant, with a sidewise glance of victory at me; but Culwin cowered gnomelike among his cushions, dissembling himself in a protective cloud of smoke.

"What's the use of denying it? You've seen everything, so of course you've seen a ghost!" his young friend persisted, talking intrepidly into the cloud. "Or, if you haven't seen one, it's only because you've seen two!"

The form of the challenge seemed to strike our host. He shot his head out of the mist with a queer tortoise-like motion he sometimes had, and blinked approvingly at Frenham.

"Yes," he suddenly flung at us on a shrill jerk of laughter; "it's only because I've seen two!"

The words were so unexpected that they dropped down and down into a fathomless silence, while we continued to stare at each other over Culwin's head, and Culwin stared at his ghosts. At length Frenham, without speaking, threw himself into the chair on the other side of the hearth, and leaned forward with his listening smile…

II

"Oh, of course they're not show ghosts—a collector wouldn't think anything of them… Don't let me raise your hopes… their one merit is their numerical strength: the exceptional fact of their being *two*. But, as against this, I'm bound to admit that at any moment I could probably have exorcized them both by asking my doctor for a prescription, or my oculist for a pair of spectacles. Only, as I never could make up my mind whether to go to the doctor or the oculist—whether I was afflicted by an optical or a digestive delusion—I left them to pursue their interesting double life, though at times they made mine exceedingly uncomfortable…

"Yes—uncomfortable; and you know how I hate to be uncomfortable! But it was part of my stupid pride, when the thing began, not to admit that I could be disturbed by the trifling matter of seeing two—

"And then I'd no reason, really, to suppose I was ill. As far as I knew I was simply bored—horribly bored. But it was part of my boredom—I remember—that I was feeling so uncommonly well, and didn't know how on earth to work off my surplus energy. I had come back from a long journey—down in South America and Mexico—and had settled down for the winter near New York, with an old aunt who had known Washington Irving and corresponded with N.P. Willis. She lived, not far from Irvington, in a damp Gothic villa, overhung by Norway spruces, and looking exactly like a memorial emblem done in hair. Her personal appearance was in keeping with this image, and her own hair—of which there was little left—might have been sacrificed to the manufacture of the emblem.

"I had just reached the end of an agitated year, with considerable arrears to make up in money and emotion; and theoretically it seemed as though my aunt's mild hospitality would be as beneficial to my nerves as to my purse. But the deuce of it was that as soon as I felt myself safe and sheltered my energy began to revive; and how was I to work it off inside of a memorial emblem? I had, at that time, the agreeable illusion that sustained intellectual effort could engage a man's whole activity; and I decided to write a great book—I forget about what. My aunt, impressed by my plan, gave up to me her Gothic library, filled with classics in black cloth and daguerrotypes of faded celebrities; and I sat down at my desk to make myself a place among their number. And to facilitate my task she lent me a cousin to copy my manuscript.

"The cousin was a nice girl, and I had an idea that a nice girl was just what I needed to restore my faith in human nature, and principally in myself. She was neither beautiful nor intelligent—poor Alice Nowell!—but it interested me to see any woman content to be so uninteresting, and I wanted to find out the secret of her content. In doing this I handled it rather rashly, and put it out of joint—oh, just for a moment! There's no fatuity in telling you this, for the poor girl had never seen anyone but cousins…

"Well, I was sorry for what I'd done, of course, and confoundedly bothered as to how I should put it straight. She was staying in the house, and one evening, after my aunt had gone to bed, she came down to the library to fetch a book she'd mislaid, like any artless heroine on the shelves behind us. She was pink-nosed and flustered, and it suddenly occurred to me that her hair, though it was fairly thick and pretty, would look exactly like my aunt's when she grew older. I was glad I had noticed this, for it made it easier for me to do what was right; and when I had found the book she hadn't lost I told her I was leaving for Europe that week.

"Europe was terribly far off in those days, and Alice knew at once what I meant. She didn't take it in the least as I'd expected—it would have been easier if she had. She held her book very tight, and turned away a moment to wind up the lamp on my desk—it had a ground glass shade with vine leaves, and glass drops around the edge, I remember. Then she came back, held out her hand, and said: 'Goodbye.' And as she said it she looked straight at me and kissed me. I had never felt anything as fresh and shy and brave as her kiss. It was worse than any reproach, and it made me ashamed to deserve a reproach from her. I said to myself: 'I'll marry her, and when my aunt dies she'll leave us this house, and I'll sit here at the desk and go on with my book; and Alice will sit over there with her embroidery and look at me as she's looking now. And life will go on like that for any number of years.' The prospect frightened me a little, but at the time it didn't frighten me as much as doing anything to hurt her; and ten minutes later she had my seal ring on her finger, and my promise that when I went abroad she should go with me.

"You'll wonder why I'm enlarging on this familiar incident. It's because the evening on which it took place was the very evening on which I first saw the queer sight I've spoken of. Being at that time an ardent believer in a necessary sequence between cause and effect I naturally tried to trace some kind of link between what had just happened to me in my aunt's library, and what was to happen a few hours later on the same night; and so the coincidence between the two events always remained in my mind.

"I went up to bed with rather a heavy heart, for I was bowed under the weight of the first good action I had ever consciously committed; and young as I was, I saw the gravity of my situation. Don't imagine from this that I had hitherto been an instrument of destruction. I had been merely a harmless young man, who had followed his bent and declined all collaboration with Providence. Now I had suddenly undertaken to promote the moral order of the world, and I felt a good deal like the trustful spectator who has given his gold watch to the conjurer, and doesn't know in what shape he'll get it back when the trick is over... Still, a glow of self-righteousness tempered my fears, and I said to myself as I undressed that when I'd got used to being good it probably wouldn't make me as nervous as it did at the start. And by the time I was in bed, and had blown out my candle, I felt that I really *was* getting used to it, and that, as far as I'd got, it was not unlike sinking down into one of my aunt's very softest wool mattresses.

"I closed my eyes on this image, and when I opened them it must have been a good deal later, for my room had grown cold, and the night was intensely still. I was waked suddenly by the feeling we all know—the feeling that there was something near me that hadn't been there when I fell asleep. I sat up and strained my eyes into the darkness. The room was pitch black, and at first I saw nothing; but gradually a vague glimmer at the foot of the bed turned into two eyes staring back at me. I couldn't see the face attached to them—on account of the darkness, I imagined—but as I looked the eyes grew more and more distinct: they gave out a light of their own.

"The sensation of being thus gazed at was far from pleasant, and you might suppose that my first impulse would have been to jump out of bed and hurl myself on the invisible figure attached to the eyes. But it wasn't—my impulse was simply to lie still… I can't say whether this was due to an immediate sense of the uncanny nature of the apparition—to the certainty that if I did jump out of bed I should hurl myself on nothing—or merely to the benumbing effect of the eyes themselves. They were the very worst eyes I've ever seen: a man's eyes—but what a man! My first thought was that he must be frightfully old. The orbits were sunk, and the thick red-lined lids hung over the eyeballs like blinds of which the cords are broken. One lid drooped a little lower than the other, with the effect of a crooked leer; and between these pulpy folds of flesh, with their scant bristle of lashes, the eyes themselves, small glassy disks with an agate-like rim about the pupils, looked like sea pebbles in the grip of a starfish.

"But the age of the eyes was not the most unpleasant thing about them. What turned me sick was their expression of vicious security. I don't know how else to describe the fact that they seemed to belong to a man who had done a lot of harm in his life, but had always kept just inside the danger lines. They were not the eyes of a coward, but of someone much too clever to take risks; and my gorge rose at their look of base astuteness. Yet even that wasn't the worst; for as we continued to scan each other I saw in them a tinge of faint derision, and felt myself to be its object.

"At that I was seized by an impulse of rage that jerked me out of bed and pitched me straight on the unseen figure at its foot. But of course there wasn't any figure there, and my fists struck at emptiness. Ashamed and cold, I groped about for a match and lit the candles. The room looked just as usual—as I had known it would; and I crawled back to bed, and blew out the lights.

"As soon as the room was dark again the eyes reappeared; and I now applied myself to explaining them on scientific principles. At first I thought the illusion might have been caused by the glow of the last embers in the chimney; but the fireplace was on the other side of my bed, and so placed that the fire could not possibly be reflected in my toilet glass, which was the only mirror in the room. Then it occurred to me that I might have been tricked by the reflection of the embers in some polished bit of wood or metal; and though I couldn't discover any object of the sort in my line of vision, I got up again, groped my way to the hearth, and covered what was left of the fire. But as soon as I was back in bed the eyes were back at its foot.

"They were an hallucination, then: that was plain. But the fact that they were not due to any external dupery didn't make them a bit pleasanter to see. For if they were a projection of my inner consciousness, what the deuce was the matter with that organ? I had gone deeply enough into the mystery of morbid pathological states to picture the conditions under which an exploring mind might lay itself open to such a midnight admonition; but I couldn't fit it to my present case. I had never felt more normal, mentally and physically; and the only unusual fact in my situation—that of having assured the happiness of an amiable girl—did not seem of a kind to summon unclean spirits about my pillow. But there were the eyes still looking at me…

"I shut mine, and tried to evoke a vision of Alice Nowell's. They were not remarkable eyes, but they were as wholesome as fresh water, and if she had had more imagination—or longer lashes—their expression might have been interesting. As it was, they did not prove very efficacious, and in a few moments I perceived that they had mysteriously changed into the eyes at the foot of the bed. It exasperated me more to feel these glaring at me through my shut lids than to see them, and I opened my eyes again and looked straight into their hateful stare…

"And so it went on all night. I can't tell you what that night was, nor how long it lasted. Have you ever lain in bed, hopelessly wide awake, and tried to keep your eyes shut, knowing that if you opened 'em you'd see something you dreaded and loathed? It sounds easy, but it's devilish hard. Those eyes hung there and drew me. I had the *vertige de l'abîme*, and their red lids were the edge of my abyss… I had known nervous hours before: hours when I'd felt the wind of danger in my neck; but never this kind of strain. It wasn't that the eyes were so awful; they hadn't the majesty of the powers of darkness. But they had—how shall I say?—a physical effect that was the equivalent of a bad smell: their look left a smear like a snail's. And I didn't see what business they had with me, anyhow—and I stared and stared, trying to find out...

"I don't know what effect they were trying to produce; but the effect they *did* produce was that of making me pack my portmanteau and bolt to town early the next morning. I left a note for my aunt, explaining that I was ill and had gone to see my doctor; and as a matter of fact I did feel uncommonly ill—the night seemed to have pumped all the blood out of me. But when I reached town I didn't go to the doctor's. I went to a friend's rooms, and threw myself on a bed, and slept for ten heavenly hours. When I woke it was the middle of the night, and I turned cold at the thought of what might be waiting for me. I sat up, shaking, and stared into the darkness; but there wasn't a break in its blessed surface, and when I saw that the eyes were not there I dropped back into another long sleep.

"I had left no word for Alice when I fled, because I meant to go back the next morning. But the next morning I was too exhausted to stir. As the day went on the exhaustion increased, instead of wearing off like the lassitude left by an ordinary night of insomnia: the effect of the eyes seemed to be cumulative, and the thought of seeing them again grew intolerable. For two days I struggled with my dread; but on the third evening I pulled myself together and decided to go back the next morning. I felt a good deal happier as soon as I'd decided, for I knew that my abrupt disappearance, and the strangeness of my not writing, must have been very painful for poor Alice. That night I went to bed with an easy mind, and fell asleep at once; but in the middle of the night I woke, and there were the eyes…

"Well, I simply couldn't face them; and instead of going back to my aunt's I bundled a few things into a trunk and jumped onto the first steamer for England. I was so dead tired when I got on board that I crawled straight into my berth, and slept most of the way over; and I can't tell you the bliss it was to wake from those long stretches of dreamless sleep and look fearlessly into the darkness, *knowing* that I shouldn't see the eyes…

"I stayed abroad for a year, and then I stayed for another; and during that time I never had a glimpse of them. That was enough reason for prolonging my stay if I'd been on a desert island. Another was, of course, that I had perfectly come to see, on the voyage over, the folly, complete impossibility, of my marrying Alice Nowell. The fact that I had been so slow in making this discovery annoyed me, and made me want to avoid explanations. The bliss of escaping at one stroke from the eyes, and from this other embarrassment, gave my freedom an extraordinary zest; and the longer I savoured it the better I liked its taste.

"The eyes had burned such a hole in my consciousness that for a long time I went on puzzling over the nature of the apparition, and wondering nervously if it would ever come back. But as time passed I lost this dread, and retained only the precision of the image. Then that faded in its turn.

"The second year found me settled in Rome, where I was planning, I believe, to write another great book—a definitive work on Etruscan influences in Italian art. At any rate, I'd found some pretext of the kind for taking a sunny apartment in the Piazza di Spagna and dabbling about indefinitely in the Forum; and there, one morning, a charming youth came to me. As he stood there in the warm light, slender and smooth and hyacinthine, he might have stepped from a ruined altar—one to Antinous, say—but he'd come instead from New York, with a letter (of all people) from Alice Nowell. The letter—the first I'd had from her since our break—was simply a line introducing her young cousin, Gilbert Noyes, and appealing to me to befriend him. It appeared, poor lad, that he 'had talent,' and 'wanted to write'; and, an obdurate family having insisted that his calligraphy should take the form of double entry, Alice had intervened to win him six months' respite, during which he was to travel on a meagre pittance, and somehow prove his ultimate ability to increase it by his pen. The quaint conditions of the test struck me first: it seemed about as conclusive as a mediaeval 'ordeal.' Then I was touched by her having sent him to me. I had always wanted to do her some service, to justify myself in my own eyes rather than hers; and here was a beautiful embodiment of my chance.

"Well, I imagine it's safe to lay down the general principle that predestined geniuses don't, as a rule, appear before one in the spring sunshine of the Forum looking like one of its banished gods. At any rate, poor Noyes wasn't a predestined genius. But he *was* beautiful to see, and charming as a comrade too.

It was only when he began to talk literature that my heart failed me. I knew all the symptoms so well—the things he had 'in him,' and the things outside him that impinged! There's the real test, after all. It was always—punctually, inevitably, with the inexorableness of a mechanical law—it was *always* the wrong thing that struck him. I grew to find a certain grim fascination in deciding in advance exactly which wrong thing he'd select; and I acquired an astonishing skill at the game…

"The worst of it was that his *bêtise* wasn't of the too obvious sort. Ladies who met him at picnics thought him intellectual; and even at dinners he passed for clever. I, who had him under the microscope, fancied now and then that he might develop some kind of a slim talent, something that he could make 'do' and be happy on; and wasn't that, after all, what I was concerned with? He was so charming—he continued to be so charming—that he called forth all my charity in support of this argument; and for the first few months I really believed there was a chance for him…

"Those months were delightful. Noyes was constantly with me, and the more I saw of him the better I liked him. His stupidity was a natural grace—it was as beautiful, really, as his eyelashes. And he was so gay, so affectionate, and so happy with me, that telling him the truth would have been about as pleasant as slitting the throat of some artless animal. At first I used to wonder what had put into that radiant head the detestable delusion that it held a brain. Then I began to see that it was simply protective mimicry—an instinctive ruse to get away from family life and an office desk. Not that Gilbert didn't—dear lad!—believe in himself. There wasn't a trace of hypocrisy in his composition. He was sure that his 'call' was irresistible, while to me it was the saving grace of his situation that it *wasn't*, and that a little money, a little leisure, a little pleasure would have turned him into an inoffensive idler. Unluckily, however, there was no hope of money, and with the grim alternative of the office desk before him he couldn't postpone his attempt at literature. The stuff he turned out was deplorable, and I see now that I knew it from the first. Still, the absurdity of deciding a man's whole future on a first trial seemed to justify me in withholding my verdict, and perhaps even in encouraging him a little, on the ground that the human plant generally needs warmth to flower.

"At any rate, I proceeded on that principle, and carried it to the point of getting his term of probation extended. When I left Rome he went with me, and we idled away a delicious summer between Capri and Venice. I said to myself: 'If he has anything in him, it will come out now; and it *did*. He was never more enchanting and enchanted. There were moments of our pilgrimage when beauty born of murmuring sound seemed actually to pass into his face—but only to issue forth in a shallow flood of the palest ink…

"Well the time came to turn off the tap; and I knew there was no hand but mine to do it. We were back in Rome, and I had taken him to stay with me, not wanting him to be alone in his dismal *pension* when he had to face the necessity of renouncing his ambition. I hadn't, of course, relied solely on my own judgment in deciding to advise him to drop literature. I had sent his stuff to various people—editors and critics—and they had always sent it back with the same chilling lack of comment. Really there was nothing on earth to say about it—

"I confess I never felt more shabbily than I did on the day when I decided to have it out with Gilbert. It was well enough to tell myself that it was my duty to knock the poor boy's hopes into splinters—but I'd like to know what act of gratuitous cruelty hasn't been justified on that plea? I've always shrunk from usurping the functions of Providence, and when I have to exercise them I decidedly prefer that it shouldn't be on an errand of destruction. Besides, in the last issue, who was I to decide, even after a year's trial, if poor Gilbert had it in him or not?

"The more I looked at the part I'd resolved to play, the less I liked it; and I liked it still less when Gilbert sat opposite me, with his head thrown back in the lamplight, just as Phil's is now… I'd been going over his last manuscript, and he knew it, and he knew that his future hung on my verdict—we'd tacitly agreed to that. The manuscript lay between us, on my table—a novel, his first novel, if you please!—and he reached over and laid his hand on it, and looked up at me with all his life in the look.

"I stood up and cleared my throat, trying to keep my eyes away from his face and on the manuscript.

"'The fact is, my dear Gilbert,' I began—

"I saw him turn pale, but he was up and facing me in an instant.

"'Oh, look here, don't take on so, my dear fellow! I'm not so awfully cut up as all that!' His hands were on my shoulders, and he was laughing down on me from his full height, with a kind of mortally stricken gaiety that drove the knife into my side.

"He was too beautifully brave for me to keep up any humbug about my duty. And it came over me suddenly how I should hurt others in hurting him: myself first, since sending him home meant losing him; but more particularly poor Alice Nowell, to whom I had so uneasily longed to prove my good faith and my immense desire to serve her. It really seemed like failing her twice to fail Gilbert—

"But my intuition was like one of those lightning flashes that encircle the whole horizon, and in the same instant I saw what I might be letting myself in for if I didn't tell the truth. I said to myself: 'I shall have him for life'—and I'd never yet seen anyone, man or woman, whom I was quite sure of wanting on those terms. Well, this impulse of egotism decided me. I was ashamed of it, and to get away from it I took a leap that landed me straight in Gilbert's arms.

"'The thing's all right, and you're all wrong!' I shouted up at him; and as he hugged me, and I laughed and shook in his incredulous clutch, I had for a minute the sense of self-complacency that is supposed to attend the footsteps of the just. Hang it all, making people happy *has* its charms—

"Gilbert, of course, was for celebrating his emancipation in some spectacular manner; but I sent him away alone to explode his emotions, and went to bed to sleep off mine. As I undressed I began to wonder what their aftertaste would be—so many of the finest don't keep! Still, I wasn't sorry, and I meant to empty the bottle, even if it *did* turn a trifle flat.

"After I got into bed I lay for a long time smiling at the memory of his eyes—his blissful eyes… Then I fell asleep, and when I woke the room was deathly cold, and I sat up with a jerk—and there were *the other eyes*…

"It was three years since I'd seen them, but I'd thought of them so often that I fancied they could never take me unawares again. Now, with their red sneer on me, I knew that I had never really believed they would come back, and that I was as defenceless as ever against them… As before, it was the insane irrelevance of their coming that made it so horrible. What the deuce were they after, to leap out at me at such a time? I had lived more or less carelessly in the years since I'd seen them, though my worst indiscretions were not dark enough to invite the searchings of their infernal glare; but at this particular moment I was really in what might have been called a state of grace; and I can't tell you how the fact added to their horror…

"But it's not enough to say they were as bad as before: they were worse. Worse by just so much as I'd learned of life in the interval; by all the damnable implications my wider experience read into them. I saw now what I hadn't seen before: that they were eyes which had grown hideous gradually, which had built up their baseness coral-wise, bit by bit, out of a series of small turpitudes slowly accumulated through the industrious years. Yes—it came to me that what made them so bad was that they'd grown bad so slowly...

"There they hung in the darkness, their swollen lids dropped across the little watery bulbs rolling loose in the orbits, and the puff of fat flesh making a muddy shadow underneath—and as their filmy stare moved with my movements, there came over me a sense of their tacit complicity, of a deep hidden understanding between us that was worse than the first shock of their strangeness. Not that I understood them; but that they made it so clear that some day I should... Yes, that was the worst part of it, decidedly; and it was the feeling that became stronger each time they came back to me...

"For they got into the damnable habit of coming back. They reminded me of vampires with a taste for young flesh, they seemed so to gloat over the taste of a good conscience. Every night for a month they came to claim their morsel of mine: since I'd made Gilbert happy they simply wouldn't loosen their fangs. The coincidence almost made me hate him, poor lad, fortuitous as I felt it to be. I puzzled over it a good deal, but couldn't find any hint of an explanation except in the chance of his association with Alice Nowell. But then the eyes had let up on me the moment I had abandoned her, so they could hardly be the emissaries of a woman scorned, even if one could have pictured poor Alice charging such spirits to avenge her. That set me thinking, and I began to wonder if they would let up on me if I abandoned Gilbert. The temptation was insidious, and I had to stiffen myself against it; but really, dear boy! he was too charming to be sacrificed to such demons. And so, after all, I never found out what they wanted…"

III

The fire crumbled, sending up a flash which threw into relief the narrator's gnarled red face under its grey-black stubble. Pressed into the hollow of the dark leather armchair, it stood out an instant like an intaglio of yellowish red-veined stone, with spots of enamel for the eyes; then the fire sank and in the shaded lamplight it became once more a dim Rembrandtish blur.

Phil Frenham, sitting in a low chair on the opposite side of the hearth, one long arm propped on the table behind him, one hand supporting his thrown-back head, and his eyes steadily fixed on his old friend's face, had not moved since the tale began. He continued to maintain his silent immobility after Culwin had ceased to speak, and it was I who, with a vague sense of disappointment at the sudden drop of the story, finally asked: "But how long did you keep on seeing them?"

Culwin, so sunk into his chair that he seemed like a heap of his own empty clothes, stirred a little, as if in surprise at my question. He appeared to have half-forgotten what he had been telling us.

"How long? Oh, off and on all that winter. It was infernal. I never got used to them. I grew really ill."

Frenham shifted his attitude silently, and as he did so his elbow struck against a small mirror in a bronze frame standing on the table behind him. He turned and changed its angle slightly; then he resumed his former attitude, his dark head thrown back on his lifted palm, his eyes intent on Culwin's face. Something in his stare embarrassed me, and as if to divert attention from it I pressed on with another question:

"And you never tried sacrificing Noyes?"

"Oh, no. The fact is I didn't have to. He did it for me, poor infatuated boy!"

"Did it for you? How do you mean?"

"He wore me out—wore everybody out. He kept on pouring out his lamentable twaddle, and hawking it up and down the place till he became a thing of terror. I tried to wean him from writing—oh, ever so gently, you understand, by throwing him with agreeable people, giving him a chance to make himself felt, to come to a sense of what he *really* had to give. I'd foreseen this solution from the beginning—felt sure that, once the first ardour of authorship was quenched, he'd drop into his place as a charming parasitic thing, the kind of chronic Cherubino for whom, in old societies, there's always a seat at table, and a shelter behind the ladies' skirts. I saw him take his place as 'the poet': the poet who doesn't write. One knows the type in every drawing room. Living in that way doesn't cost much—I'd worked it all out in my mind, and felt sure that, with a little help, he could manage it for the next few years; and meanwhile he'd be sure to marry. I saw him married to a widow, rather older, with a good cook and a well-run house. And I actually had my eye on the widow... Meanwhile I did everything to facilitate the transition—lent him money to ease his conscience, introduced him to pretty women to make him forget his vows. But nothing would do him: he had but one idea in his beautiful obstinate head. He wanted the laurel and not the rose, and he kept on repeating Gautier's axiom, and battering and filing at his limp prose till he'd spread it out over Lord knows how many thousand sloppy pages. Now and then he would send a pailful to a publisher, and of course it would always come back.

"At first it didn't matter—he thought he was 'misunderstood.' He took the attitudes of genius, and whenever an opus came home he wrote another to keep it company. Then he had a reaction of despair, and accused me of deceiving him, and Lord knows what. I got angry at that, and told him it was he who had deceived himself. He'd come to me determined to write, and I'd done my best to help him. That was the extent of my offence, and I'd done it for his cousin's sake, not his.

"That seemed to strike home, and he didn't answer for a minute. Then he said: 'My time's up and my money's up. What do you think I'd better do?'

"'I think you'd better not be an ass,' I said.

"He turned red, and asked: 'What do you mean by being an ass?'

"I took a letter from my desk and held it out to him.

"'I mean refusing this offer of Mrs. Ellinger's: to be her secretary at a salary of five thousand dollars. There may be a lot more in it than that.'

"He flung out his hand with a violence that struck the letter from mine. 'Oh, I know well enough what's in it!' he said, scarlet to the roots of his hair.

"'And what's your answer, if you know?' I asked.

"He made none at the minute, but turned away slowly to the door. There, with his hand on the threshold, he stopped to ask, almost under his breath: 'Then you really think my stuff's no good?'

"I was tired and exasperated, and I laughed. I don't defend my laugh—it was in wretched taste. But I must plead in extenuation that the boy was a fool, and that I'd done my best for him—I really had.

"He went out of the room, shutting the door quietly after him. That afternoon I left for Frascati, where I'd promised to spend the Sunday with some friends. I was glad to escape from Gilbert, and by the same token, as I learned that night, I had also escaped from the eyes. I dropped into the same lethargic sleep that had come to me before when their visitations ceased; and when I woke the next morning, in my peaceful painted room above the ilexes, I felt the utter weariness and deep relief that always followed on that repairing slumber. I put in two blessed nights at Frascati, and when I got back to my rooms in Rome I found that Gilbert had gone… Oh, nothing tragic had happened—the episode never rose to *that.* He'd simply packed his manuscripts and left for America—for his family and the Wall Street desk. He left a decent little note to tell me of his decision, and behaved altogether, in the circumstances, as little like a fool as it's possible for a fool to behave…"

IV

Culwin paused again, and again Frenham sat motionless, the dusky contour of his young head reflected in the mirror at his back.

"And what became of Noyes afterward?" I finally asked, still disquieted by a sense of incompleteness, by the need of some connecting thread between the parallel lines of the tale.

Culwin twitched his shoulders. "Oh, nothing became of him—because he became nothing. There could be no question of 'becoming' about it. He vegetated in an office, I believe, and finally got a clerkship in a consulate, and married drearily in China. I saw him once in Hong Kong, years afterward. He was fat and hadn't shaved. I was told he drank. He didn't recognize me."

"And the eyes?" I asked, after another pause which Frenham's continued silence made oppressive.

Culwin, stroking his chin, blinked at me meditatively through the shadows. "I never saw them after my last talk with Gilbert. Put two and two together if you can. For my part, I haven't found the link."

He rose stiffly, his hands in his pockets, and walked over to the table on which reviving drinks had been set out.

"You must be parched after this dry tale. Here, help yourself, my dear fellow. Here, Phil—" He turned back to the hearth.

Frenham still sat in his low chair, making no

response to his host's hospitable summons. But as Culwin advanced toward him, their eyes met in a long look; after which, to my intense surprise, the young man, turning suddenly in his seat, flung his arms across the table, and dropped his face upon them.

Culwin, at the unexpected gesture, stopped short, a flush on his face.

"Phil—what the deuce? Why, have the eyes scared *you*? My dear boy—my dear fellow—I never had such a tribute to my literary ability, never!"

He broke into a chuckle at the thought, and halted on the hearth rug, his hands still in his pockets, gazing down in honest perplexity at the youth's bowed head. Then, as Frenham still made no answer, he moved a step or two nearer.

"Cheer up, my dear Phil! It's years since I've seen them—apparently I've done nothing lately bad enough to call them out of chaos. Unless my present evocation of them has made *you* see them; which would be their worst stroke yet!"

His bantering appeal quivered off into an uneasy laugh, and he moved still nearer, bending over Frenham, and laying his gouty hands on the lad's shoulders.

"Phil, my dear boy, really—what's the matter? Why don't you answer? *Have* you seen the eyes?"

Frenham's face was still pressed against his arms, and from where I stood behind Culwin I saw the latter, as if under the rebuff of this unaccountable attitude, draw back slowly from his friend. As he did so, the light of the lamp on the table fell full on his perplexed congested face, and I caught its sudden reflection in the mirror behind Frenham's head.

Culwin saw the reflection also. He paused, his face level with the mirror, as if scarcely recognizing the countenance in it as his own. But as he looked his expression gradually changed, and for an appreciable space of time he and the image in the glass confronted each other with a glare of slowly gathering hate. Then Culwin let go of Frenham's shoulders, and drew back a step, covering his eyes with his hands...

Frenham, his face still hidden, did not stir.

THE MASK

Robert W. Chambers

CAMILLA: You, sir, should unmask.
STRANGER: Indeed?
CASSILDA: Indeed it's time. We all have laid aside disguise but you.
STRANGER: I wear no mask.
CAMILLA: (*Terrified, aside to Cassilda.*) No mask? No mask!

THE KING IN YELLOW,
ACT I, SCENE II

I

ALTHOUGH I KNEW NOTHING of chemistry, I listened fascinated. He picked up an Easter lily which Geneviève had brought that morning from Notre Dame, and dropped it into the basin. Instantly the liquid lost its crystalline clearness. For a second the lily was enveloped in a milk-white foam, which disappeared, leaving the fluid opalescent. Changing tints of orange and crimson played over the surface, and then what seemed to be a ray of pure sunlight struck through from the bottom where the lily was resting. At the same instant he plunged his hand into the basin and drew out the flower. "There is no danger," he explained, "if you choose the right moment. That golden ray is the signal."

He held the lily toward me, and I took it in my hand. It had turned to stone, to the purest marble.

"You see," he said, "it is without a flaw. What sculptor could reproduce it?"

The marble was white as snow, but in its depths the veins of the lily were tinged with palest azure, and a faint flush lingered deep in its heart.

"Don't ask me the reason of that," he smiled, noticing my wonder. "I have no idea why the veins and heart are tinted, but they always are. Yesterday I tried one of Geneviève's goldfish—there it is."

The fish looked as if sculptured in marble. But if you held it to the light the stone was beautifully veined with a faint blue, and from somewhere within came a rosy light like the tint which slumbers in an opal. I looked into the basin. Once more it seemed filled with clearest crystal.

"If I should touch it now?" I demanded.

"I don't know," he replied, "but you had better not try."

"There is one thing I'm curious about," I said, "and that is where the ray of sunlight came from."

"It looked like a sunbeam true enough," he said. "I don't know, it always comes when I immerse any living thing. Perhaps," he continued, smiling, "perhaps it is the vital spark of the creature escaping to the source from whence it came."

I saw he was mocking, and threatened him with a mahlstick, but he only laughed and changed the subject.

"Stay to lunch. Geneviève will be here directly."

"I saw her going to early mass," I said, "and she looked as fresh and sweet as that lily—before you destroyed it."

"Do you think I destroyed it?" said Boris gravely.

"Destroyed, preserved, how can we tell?"

We sat in the corner of a studio near his unfinished group of the "Fates." He leaned back on the sofa, twirling a sculptor's chisel and squinting at his work.

"By the way," he said, "I have finished pointing up that old academic Ariadne, and I suppose it will have to go to the Salon. It's all I have ready this year, but after the success the 'Madonna' brought me I feel ashamed to send a thing like that."

The "Madonna," an exquisite marble for which Geneviève had sat, had been the sensation of last year's Salon. I looked at the Ariadne. It was a magnificent piece of technical work, but I agreed with Boris that the world would expect something better of him than that. Still, it was impossible now to think of finishing in time for the Salon that splendid terrible group half shrouded in the marble behind me. The "Fates" would have to wait.

We were proud of Boris Yvain. We claimed him and he claimed us on the strength of his having been born in America, although his father was French and his mother was a Russian. Everyone in the Beaux Arts called him Boris. And yet there were only two of us whom he addressed in the same familiar way—Jack Scott and myself.

Perhaps my being in love with Geneviève had something to do with his affection for me. Not that it had ever been acknowledged between us. But after all was settled, and she had told me with tears in her eyes that it was Boris whom she loved, I went over to his house and congratulated him. The perfect cordiality of that interview did not deceive either of us, I always believed, although to one at least it was a great comfort. I do not think he and Geneviève ever spoke of the matter together, but Boris knew.

Geneviève was lovely. The Madonna-like purity of her face might have been inspired by the Sanctus in Gounod's Mass. But I was always glad when she changed that mood for what we called her "April Manœuvres." She was often as variable as an April day. In the morning grave, dignified and sweet, at noon laughing, capricious, at evening whatever one least expected. I preferred her so rather than in that Madonna-like tranquillity which stirred the depths of my heart. I was dreaming of Geneviève when he spoke again.

"What do you think of my discovery, Alec?"

"I think it wonderful."

"I shall make no use of it, you know, beyond satisfying my own curiosity so far as may be, and the secret will die with me."

"It would be rather a blow to sculpture, would it not? We painters lose more than we ever gain by photography."

Boris nodded, playing with the edge of the chisel.

"This new vicious discovery would corrupt the world of art. No, I shall never confide the secret to anyone," he said slowly.

It would be hard to find anyone less informed about such phenomena than myself; but of course I had heard of mineral springs so saturated with silica that the leaves and twigs which fell into them were turned to stone after a time. I dimly comprehended the process, how the silica replaced the vegetable matter, atom by atom, and the result was a duplicate of the object in stone. This, I confess, had never interested me greatly, and as for the ancient fossils thus produced, they disgusted me. Boris, it appeared, feeling curiosity instead of repugnance, had investigated the subject, and had accidentally stumbled on a solution which, attacking the immersed object with a ferocity unheard of, in a second did the work of years. This was all I could make out of the strange story he had just been telling me. He spoke again after a long silence.

"I am almost frightened when I think what I have found. Scientists would go mad over the discovery. It was so simple too; it discovered itself. When I think of that formula, and that new element precipitated in metallic scales—"

"What new element?"

"Oh, I haven't thought of naming it, and I don't believe I ever shall. There are enough precious metals now in the world to cut throats over."

I pricked up my ears. "Have you struck gold, Boris?"

"No, better—but see here, Alec!" he laughed, starting up. "You and I have all we need in this world. Ah! how sinister and covetous you look already!" I laughed too, and told him I was devoured by the desire for gold, and we had better talk of something else; so when Geneviève came in shortly after, we had turned our backs on alchemy.

Geneviève was dressed in silvery grey from head to foot. The light glinted along the soft curves of her fair hair as she turned her cheek to Boris; then she saw me and returned my greeting. She had never before failed to blow me a kiss from the tips of her white fingers, and I promptly complained of the omission. She smiled and held out her hand, which dropped almost before it had touched mine; then she said, looking at Boris—

"You must ask Alec to stay for luncheon." This also was something new. She had always asked me herself until today.

"I did," said Boris shortly.

"And you said yes, I hope?" She turned to me with a charming conventional smile. I might have been an acquaintance of the day before yesterday. I made her a low bow. "*J'avais bien l'honneur, madame*," but refusing to take up our usual bantering tone, she murmured a hospitable commonplace and disappeared. Boris and I looked at one another.

"I had better go home, don't you think?" I asked.

"Hanged if I know," he replied frankly.

While we were discussing the advisability of my departure Geneviève reappeared in the doorway without her bonnet. She was wonderfully beautiful, but her colour was too deep and her lovely eyes were too bright. She came straight up to me and took my arm.

"Luncheon is ready. Was I cross, Alec? I thought I had a headache, but I haven't. Come here, Boris"; and she slipped her other arm through his. "Alec knows that after you there is no one in the world whom I like as well as I like him, so if he sometimes feels snubbed it won't hurt him."

"*À la bonheur!*" I cried, "who says there are no thunderstorms in April?"

"Are you ready?" chanted Boris. "Aye ready"; and arm-in-arm we raced into the dining room,

Seattle Public Library
Beacon Hill Branch
(206) 684-4711

04/13/23 01:37PM

Borrower # ****23

The food of Oaxaca : recipes and stories
0010103879911 Date Due: 05/04/23
acbk

The rough guide to Italy.
0010107550435 Date Due: 05/04/23
acbk

The lost daughter /
0010103448063 Date Due: 05/04/23
acbk

American midnight : tales of the dark /
0010104929954 Date Due: 05/04/23
acbk

TOTAL ITEMS: 4

Visit us on the Web at www.spl.org

scandalizing the servants. After all we were not so much to blame; Geneviève was eighteen, Boris was twenty-three, and I not quite twenty-one.

II

Some work that I was doing about this time on the decorations for Geneviève's boudoir kept me constantly at the quaint little hotel in the Rue Sainte-Cécile. Boris and I in those days laboured hard but as we pleased, which was fitfully, and we all three, with Jack Scott, idled a great deal together.

One quiet afternoon I had been wandering alone over the house examining curios, prying into odd corners, bringing out sweetmeats and cigars from strange hiding places, and at last I stopped in the bathing room. Boris, all over clay, stood there washing his hands.

The room was built of rose-coloured marble excepting the floor, which was tessellated in rose and grey. In the centre was a square pool sunken below the surface of the floor; steps led down into it, sculptured pillars supported a frescoed ceiling. A delicious marble Cupid appeared to have just alighted on his pedestal at the upper end of the room. The whole interior was Boris's work and mine. Boris, in his working clothes of white canvas, scraped the traces of clay and red modelling wax from his handsome hands, and coquetted over his shoulder with the Cupid.

"I see you," he insisted, "don't try to look the other way and pretend not to see me. You know who made you, little humbug!"

It was always my role to interpret Cupid's sentiments in these conversations, and when my turn came I responded in such a manner, that Boris seized my arm and dragged me toward the pool, declaring he would duck me. Next instant he dropped my arm and turned pale. "Good God!" he said, "I forgot the pool is full of the solution!"

I shivered a little, and dryly advised him to remember better where he had stored the precious liquid.

"In Heaven's name, why do you keep a small lake of that gruesome stuff here of all places?" I asked.

"I want to experiment on something large," he replied.

"On me, for instance?"

"Ah! that came too close for jesting; but I do want to watch the action of that solution on a more highly organized living body; there is that big white rabbit," he said, following me into the studio.

Jack Scott, wearing a paint-stained jacket, came wandering in, appropriated all the Oriental sweetmeats he could lay his hands on, looted the cigarette case, and finally he and Boris disappeared together to visit the Luxembourg Gallery, where a new silver bronze by Rodin and a landscape of Monet's were claiming the exclusive attention of artistic France. I went back to the studio, and resumed my work. It was a Renaissance screen, which Boris wanted me to paint for Geneviève's boudoir. But the small boy who was unwillingly dawdling through a series of poses for it, today refused all bribes to be good. He never rested an instant in the same position, and inside of five minutes I had as many different outlines of the little beggar.

"Are you posing, or are you executing a song and dance, my friend?" I inquired.

"Whichever monsieur pleases," he replied, with an angelic smile.

Of course I dismissed him for the day, and of course I paid him for the full time, that being the way we spoil our models.

After the young imp had gone, I made a few perfunctory daubs at my work, but was so thoroughly out of humour, that it took me the rest of the afternoon to undo the damage I had done, so at last I scraped my palette, stuck my brushes in a bowl of black soap, and strolled into the smoking room. I really believe that, excepting Geneviève's apartments, no room in the house was so free from the perfume of tobacco as this one. It was a queer chaos of odds and ends, hung with threadbare tapestry. A sweet-toned old spinet in good repair stood by the window. There were stands of weapons, some old and dull, others bright and modern, festoons of Indian and Turkish armour over the mantel, two or three good pictures, and a pipe rack. It was here that we used to come for new sensations in smoking. I doubt if any type of pipe ever existed which was not represented in that rack. When we had selected one, we immediately carried it somewhere else and smoked it; for the place was, on the whole, more gloomy and less inviting than any in the house. But this afternoon, the twilight was very soothing, the rugs and skins on the floor looked brown and soft and drowsy; the big couch was piled with cushions—I found my pipe and curled up there for an unaccustomed smoke in the smoking room. I had chosen one with a long flexible stem, and lighting it fell to dreaming. After a while it went out, but I did not stir. I dreamed on and presently fell asleep.

I awoke to the saddest music I had ever heard. The room was quite dark, I had no idea what time it was. A ray of moonlight silvered one edge of the old spinet, and the polished wood seemed to exhale the sounds as perfume floats above a box of sandalwood. Someone rose in the darkness, and came away weeping quietly, and I was fool enough to cry out "Geneviève!"

She dropped at my voice, and I had time to curse myself while I made a light and tried to raise her from the floor. She shrank away with a murmur of pain. She was very quiet, and asked for Boris. I carried her to the divan, and went to look for him, but he was not in the house, and the servants were gone to bed. Perplexed and anxious, I hurried back to Geneviève. She lay where I had left her, looking very white.

"I can't find Boris nor any of the servants," I said.

"I know," she answered faintly, "Boris has gone to Ept with Mr. Scott. I did not remember when I sent you for him just now."

"But he can't get back in that case before tomorrow afternoon, and—are you hurt? Did I frighten you into falling? What an awful fool I am, but I was only half awake."

"Boris thought you had gone home before dinner. Do please excuse us for letting you stay here all this time."

"I have had a long nap," I laughed, "so sound that I did not know whether I was still asleep or not when I found myself staring at a figure that was moving toward me, and called out your name. Have you been trying the old spinet? You must have played very softly."

I would tell a thousand more lies worse than that one to see the look of relief that came into her face. She smiled adorably, and said in her natural voice: "Alec, I tripped on that wolf's head, and I think my ankle is sprained. Please call Marie, and then go home."

I did as she bade me, and left her there when the maid came in.

III

At noon next day when I called, I found Boris walking restlessly about his studio.

"Geneviève is asleep just now," he told me, "the sprain is nothing, but why should she have such a high fever? The doctor can't account for it; or else he will not," he muttered.

"Geneviève has a fever?" I asked.

"I should say so, and has actually been a little light-headed at intervals all night. The idea!—gay little Geneviève, without a care in the world—and she keeps saying her heart's broken, and she wants to die!"

My own heart stood still.

Boris leaned against the door of his studio, looking down, his hands in his pockets, his kind, keen eyes clouded, a new line of trouble drawn "over the mouth's good mark, that made the smile." The maid had orders to summon him the instant Geneviève opened her eyes. We waited and waited, and Boris, growing restless, wandered about, fussing with modelling wax and red clay. Suddenly he started for the next room. "Come and see my rose-coloured bath full of death!" he cried.

"Is it death?" I asked, to humour his mood.

"You are not prepared to call it life, I suppose," he answered. As he spoke he plucked a solitary goldfish squirming and twisting out of its globe. "We'll send this one after the other—wherever that is," he said. There was feverish excitement in his voice. A dull weight of fever lay on my limbs and on my brain as I followed him to the fair crystal pool with its pink-tinted sides; and he dropped the creature in. Falling, its scales flashed with a hot orange gleam in its angry twistings and contortions; the moment it struck the liquid it became rigid and sank heavily to the bottom. Then came the milky foam, the splendid hues radiating on the surface and then the shaft of pure serene light broke through from seemingly infinite depths. Boris plunged in his hand and drew out an exquisite marble thing, blue-veined, rose-tinted, and glistening with opalescent drops.

"Child's play," he muttered, and looked wearily, longingly at me—as if I could answer such questions! But Jack Scott came in and entered into the "game," as he called it, with ardour. Nothing would do but to try the experiment on the white rabbit then and there. I was willing that Boris should find distraction from his cares, but I hated to see the life go out of a warm, living creature and I declined to be present. Picking up a book at random, I sat down in the studio to read. Alas! I had found *The King in Yellow*. After a few moments, which seemed ages, I was putting it away with a nervous shudder, when Boris and Jack came in bringing their marble rabbit. At the same time the bell rang above, and a cry came from the sickroom. Boris was gone like a flash, and the next moment he called, "Jack, run for the doctor; bring him back with you. Alec, come here."

I went and stood at her door. A frightened maid came out in haste and ran away to fetch some remedy. Geneviève, sitting bolt upright, with crimson cheeks and glittering eyes, babbled incessantly and resisted Boris's gentle restraint. He called me to help. At my first touch she sighed and sank back, closing her eyes, and then—then—as we still bent above her, she opened them again, looked straight into Boris's face—poor fever-crazed girl!—and told her secret. At the same instant our three lives turned into new channels; the bond that held us so long together snapped for ever and a new bond was forged in its place, for she had spoken my name, and as the fever tortured her, her heart poured out its load of hidden sorrow. Amazed and dumb I bowed my head, while my face burned like a live coal, and the blood surged in my ears, stupefying me with its clamour. Incapable of movement, incapable of speech, I listened to her feverish words in an agony of shame and sorrow.

I could not silence her, I could not look at Boris. Then I felt an arm upon my shoulder, and Boris turned a bloodless face to mine.

"It is not your fault, Alec; don't grieve so if she loves you—" but he could not finish; and as the doctor stepped swiftly into the room, saying "Ah, the fever!" I seized Jack Scott and hurried him to the street, saying, "Boris would rather be alone." We crossed the street to our own apartments, and that night, seeing I was going to be ill too, he went for the doctor again. The last thing I recollect with any distinctness was hearing Jack say, "For Heaven's sake, doctor, what ails him, to wear a face like that?" and I thought of *The King in Yellow* and the Pallid Mask.

I was very ill, for the strain of two years which I had endured since that fatal May morning when Geneviève murmured, "I love you, but I think I love Boris best," told on me at last. I had never imagined that it could become more than I could endure. Outwardly tranquil, I had deceived myself. Although the inward battle raged night after night, and I, lying alone in my room, cursed myself for rebellious thoughts unloyal to Boris and unworthy of Geneviève, the morning always brought relief, and

I returned to Geneviève and to my dear Boris with a heart washed clean by the tempests of the night.

Never in word or deed or thought while with them had I betrayed my sorrow even to myself.

The mask of self-deception was no longer a mask for me, it was a part of me. Night lifted it, laying bare the stifled truth below; but there was no one to see except myself, and when the day broke the mask fell back again of its own accord. These thoughts passed through my troubled mind as I lay sick, but they were hopelessly entangled with visions of white creatures, heavy as stone, crawling about in Boris's basin—of the wolf's head on the rug, foaming and snapping at Geneviève, who lay smiling beside it. I thought, too, of the King in Yellow wrapped in the fantastic colours of his tattered mantle, and that bitter cry of Cassilda, "Not upon us, oh King, not upon us!" Feverishly I struggled to put it from me, but I saw the lake of Hali, thin and blank, without a ripple or wind to stir it, and I saw the towers of Carcosa behind the moon. Aldebaran, the Hyades, Alar, Hastur, glided through the cloud rifts which fluttered and flapped as they passed like the scolloped tatters of the King in Yellow. Among all these, one sane thought persisted. It never wavered, no matter what else was going on in my disordered mind, that my chief reason for existing was to meet some requirement of Boris and Geneviève. What this obligation was, its nature, was never clear; sometimes it seemed to be protection, sometimes support, through a great crisis. Whatever it seemed to be for the time, its weight rested only on me, and I was never so ill or so weak that I did not respond with my whole soul. There were always crowds of faces about me, mostly strange, but a few I recognized, Boris among them. Afterward they told me that this could not have been, but I know that once at least he bent over me. It was only a touch, a faint echo of his voice, then the clouds settled back on my senses, and I lost him, but he *did* stand there and bend over me *once* at least.

At last, one morning I awoke to find the sunlight falling across my bed, and Jack Scott reading beside me. I had not strength enough to speak aloud, neither could I think, much less remember, but I could smile feebly, as Jack's eye met mine, and when he jumped up and asked eagerly if I wanted anything, I could whisper, "Yes—Boris." Jack moved to the head of my bed, and leaned down to arrange my pillow: I did not see his face, but he answered heartily, "You must wait, Alec; you are too weak to see even Boris."

I waited and I grew strong; in a few days I was able to see whom I would, but meanwhile I had thought and remembered. From the moment when all the past grew clear again in my mind, I never doubted what I should do when the time came, and I felt sure that Boris would have resolved upon the same course so far as he was concerned; as for what pertained to me alone, I knew he would see that also as I did. I no longer asked for anyone. I never inquired why no message came from them; why during the week I lay there, waiting and growing stronger, I never heard their name spoken. Preoccupied with my own searchings for the right way, and with my feeble but determined fight against despair, I simply acquiesced in Jack's reticence, taking for granted that he was afraid to speak of them, lest I should turn unruly and insist on seeing them. Meanwhile I said over and over to myself, how would it be when life began again for us all? We would take up our relations exactly as they were before Geneviève fell ill. Boris and I would look into each other's eyes, and there would be neither rancour nor cowardice nor mistrust in that glance. I would be with them again for a little while in the dear intimacy of their home, and then, without pretext or explanation, I would disappear from their lives for ever. Boris would know; Geneviève—the only comfort was that she would never know. It seemed, as I thought it over, that I had found the meaning of that sense of obligation which had persisted all through my delirium, and the only possible answer to it. So, when I was quite ready, I beckoned Jack to me one day, and said—

"Jack, I want Boris at once; and take my dearest greeting to Geneviève..."

When at last he made me understand that they were both dead, I fell into a wild rage that tore all my little convalescent strength to atoms. I raved and cursed myself into a relapse, from which I crawled forth some weeks afterward a boy of twenty-one who believed that his youth was gone for ever. I seemed to be past the capability of further suffering, and one day when Jack handed me a letter and the keys to Boris's house, I took them without a tremor and asked him to tell me all. It was cruel of me to ask him, but there was no help for it, and he leaned wearily on his thin hands, to reopen the wound which could never entirely heal. He began very quietly—

"Alec, unless you have a clue that I know nothing about, you will not be able to explain any more than I what has happened. I suspect that you would rather not hear these details, but you must learn them, else I would spare you the relation. God knows I wish I could be spared the telling. I shall use few words.

"That day when I left you in the doctor's care and came back to Boris, I found him working on the 'Fates.' Geneviève, he said, was sleeping under the influence of drugs. She had been quite out of her mind, he said. He kept on working, not talking any more, and I watched him. Before long, I saw that the third figure of the group—the one looking straight ahead, out over the world—bore his face; not as you ever saw it, but as it looked then and to the end. This is one thing for which I should like to find an explanation, but I never shall.

"Well, he worked and I watched him in silence, and we went on that way until nearly midnight. Then we heard the door open and shut sharply, and a swift rush in the next room. Boris sprang through the doorway and I followed; but we were too late. She lay at the bottom of the pool, her hands across her breast. Then Boris shot himself through the heart." Jack stopped speaking, drops of sweat stood under his eyes, and his thin cheeks twitched. "I carried Boris to his room. Then I went back and let that hellish fluid out of the pool, and turning on all the water, washed the marble clean of every drop. When at length I dared descend the steps, I found her lying there as white as snow. At last, when I had decided what was best to do, I went into the laboratory, and first emptied the solution in the basin into the waste pipe; then I poured the contents of every jar and bottle after it. There was wood in the fireplace, so I built a fire, and breaking the locks of Boris's cabinet I burnt every paper, notebook and letter that I found there. With a mallet from the studio I smashed to pieces all the empty bottles, then loading them into a coal scuttle, I carried them to the cellar and threw them over the red-hot bed of the furnace. Six times I made the journey, and at last, not a vestige remained of anything which might again aid in seeking for the formula which Boris had found. Then at last I dared call the doctor. He is a good man, and together we struggled to keep it from the public. Without him I never could have succeeded. At last we got the servants paid and sent away into the country, where old Rosier keeps them quiet with stories of Boris's and Geneviève's travels in distant lands, from whence they will not return for years. We buried Boris in the little cemetery of Sèvres. The doctor is a good creature, and knows when to pity a man who can bear no more. He gave his certificate of heart disease and asked no questions of me."

Then, lifting his head from his hands, he said, "Open the letter, Alec; it is for us both."

I tore it open. It was Boris's will dated a year before. He left everything to Geneviève, and in case of her dying childless, I was to take control of the house in the Rue Sainte-Cécile, and Jack Scott the management at Ept. On our deaths the property reverted to his mother's family in Russia, with the exception of the sculptured marbles executed by himself. These he left to me.

The page blurred under our eyes, and Jack got up and walked to the window. Presently he returned and sat down again. I dreaded to hear what he was going to say, but he spoke with the same simplicity and gentleness.

"Geneviève lies before the Madonna in the marble room. The Madonna bends tenderly above her, and Geneviève smiles back into that calm face that never would have been except for her."

His voice broke, but he grasped my hand, saying, "Courage, Alec." Next morning he left for Ept to fulfil his trust.

IV

The same evening I took the keys and went into the house I had known so well. Everything was in order, but the silence was terrible. Though I went twice to the door of the marble room, I could not force myself to enter. It was beyond my strength. I went into the smoking room and sat down before the spinet. A small lace handkerchief lay on the keys, and I turned away, choking. It was plain I could not stay, so I locked every door, every window, and the three front and back gates, and went away. Next morning Alcide packed my valise, and leaving him in charge of my apartments I took the Orient Express for Constantinople. During the two years that I wandered through the East, at first, in our letters, we never mentioned Geneviève and Boris, but gradually their names crept in. I recollect particularly a passage in one of Jack's letters replying to one of mine—

"What you tell me of seeing Boris bending over you while you lay ill, and feeling his touch on your face, and hearing his voice, of course troubles me. This that you describe must have happened a fortnight after he died. I say to myself that you were dreaming, that it was part of your delirium, but the explanation does not satisfy me, nor would it you."

Toward the end of the second year a letter came from Jack to me in India so unlike anything that I had ever known of him that I decided to return at once to Paris. He wrote: "I am well, and sell all my pictures as artists do who have no need of money. I have not a care of my own, but I am more restless than if I had. I am unable to shake off a strange anxiety about you. It is not apprehension, it is rather a breathless expectancy—of what, God knows! I can only say it is wearing me out. Nights I dream always of you and Boris. I can never recall anything afterward, but I wake in the morning with my heart beating, and all day the excitement increases until I fall asleep at night to recall the same experience. I am quite exhausted by it, and have determined to break up this morbid condition. I must see you. Shall I go to Bombay, or will you come to Paris?"

I telegraphed him to expect me by the next steamer.

When we met I thought he had changed very little; I, he insisted, looked in splendid health. It was good to hear his voice again, and as we sat and chatted about what life still held for us, we felt that it was pleasant to be alive in the bright spring weather.

We stayed in Paris together a week, and then I went for a week to Ept with him, but first of all we went to the cemetery at Sèvres, where Boris lay.

"Shall we place the 'Fates' in the little grove above him?" Jack asked, and I answered—

"I think only the 'Madonna' should watch over Boris's grave." But Jack was none the better for my homecoming. The dreams of which he could not retain even the least definite outline continued, and he said that at times the sense of breathless expectancy was suffocating.

"You see I do you harm and not good," I said. "Try a change without me." So he started alone for a ramble among the Channel Islands, and I went back to Paris. I had not yet entered Boris's house, now mine, since my return, but I knew it must be done. It had been kept in order by Jack; there were servants there, so I gave up my own apartment and went there to live. Instead of the agitation I had feared, I found myself able to paint there tranquilly. I visited all the rooms—all but one. I could not bring myself to enter the marble room where Geneviève lay, and yet I felt the longing growing daily to look upon her face, to kneel beside her.

One April afternoon, I lay dreaming in the smoking room, just as I had lain two years before, and mechanically I looked among the tawny Eastern rugs for the wolfskin. At last I distinguished the pointed ears and flat cruel head, and I thought of my dream where I saw Geneviève lying beside it. The helmets still hung against the threadbare tapestry, among them the old Spanish morion which I remembered Geneviève had once put on when we were amusing ourselves with the ancient bits of mail. I turned my eyes to the spinet; every yellow key seemed eloquent of her caressing hand, and I rose, drawn by the strength of my life's passion to the sealed door of the marble room. The heavy doors swung inward under my trembling hands. Sunlight poured through the window, tipping with gold the wings of Cupid, and lingered like a nimbus over the brows of the Madonna. Her tender face bent in compassion over a marble form so exquisitely pure that I knelt and signed myself. Geneviève lay in the shadow under the Madonna, and yet, through her white arms, I saw the pale azure vein, and beneath her softly clasped hands the folds of her dress were tinged with rose, as if from some faint warm light within her breast.

Bending, with a breaking heart, I touched the marble drapery with my lips, then crept back into the silent house.

A maid came and brought me a letter, and I sat down in the little conservatory to read it; but as I was about to break the seal, seeing the girl lingering, I asked her what she wanted.

She stammered something about a white rabbit that had been caught in the house, and asked what should be done with it. I told her to let it loose in the walled garden behind the house, and opened my letter. It was from Jack, but so incoherent that I thought he must have lost his reason. It was nothing but a series of prayers to me not to leave the house until he could get back; he could not tell me why, there were the dreams, he said—he could explain nothing, but he was sure that I must not leave the house in the Rue Sainte-Cécile.

As I finished reading I raised my eyes and saw the same maidservant standing in the doorway holding a glass dish in which two goldfish were swimming: "Put them back into the tank and tell me what you mean by interrupting me," I said.

With a half-suppressed whimper she emptied water and fish into an aquarium at the end of the conservatory, and turning to me asked my permission to leave my service. She said people were playing tricks on her, evidently with a design of getting her into trouble; the marble rabbit had been stolen and a live one had been brought into the house; the two beautiful marble fish were gone, and she had just found those common live things flopping on the dining-room floor. I reassured her and sent her away, saying I would look about myself. I went into the studio; there was nothing there but my canvases and some casts, except the marble of the Easter lily. I saw it on a table across the room. Then I strode angrily over to it. But the flower I lifted from the table was fresh and fragile and filled the air with perfume.

Then suddenly I comprehended, and sprang through the hallway to the marble room. The doors flew open, the sunlight streamed into my face, and through it, in a heavenly glory, the Madonna smiled, as Geneviève lifted her flushed face from her marble couch and opened her sleepy eyes.

HOME

Shirley Jackson

ETHEL SLOANE was whistling to herself as she got out of her car and splashed across the sidewalk to the doorway of the hardware store. She was wearing a new raincoat and solid boots, and one day of living in the country had made her weather-wise. "This rain can't last," she told the hardware clerk confidently. "This time of year it never lasts."

The clerk nodded tactfully. One day in the country had been enough for Ethel Sloane to become acquainted with most of the local people; she had been into the hardware store several times— "so many odd things you never expect you're going to need in an old house"—and into the post office to leave their new address, and into the grocery to make it clear that all the Sloane grocery business was going to come their way, and into the bank and into the gas station and into the little library and even as far as the door of the barbershop ("… and you'll be seeing my husband Jim Sloane in a day or so!"). Ethel Sloane liked having bought the old Sanderson place, and she liked walking the single street of the village, and most of all she liked knowing that people knew who she was.

"They make you feel at home right away, as though you were born not half a mile from here," she explained to her husband, Jim.

Privately she thought that the storekeepers in the village might show a little more alacrity in remembering her name; she had probably brought more business to the little stores in the village than any of them had seen for a year past. They're not outgoing people, she told herself reassuringly. It takes a while for them to get over being suspicious; we've been here in the house for only two days.

"First, I want to get the name of a good plumber," she said to the clerk in the hardware store. Ethel Sloane was a great believer in getting information directly from the local people; the plumbers listed in the phone book might be competent enough, but the local people always knew who would suit; Ethel

Sloane had no intention of antagonizing the villagers by hiring an unpopular plumber. "And closet hooks," she said. "My husband, Jim, turns out to be just as good a handyman as he is a writer." Always tell them your business, she thought, then they don't have to ask.

"I suppose the best one for plumbing would be Will Watson," the clerk said. "He does most of the plumbing around. You drive down the Sanderson road in this rain?"

"Of course." Ethel Sloane was surprised. "I had all kinds of things to do in the village."

"Creek's pretty high. They say that sometimes when the creek is high—"

"The bridge held our moving truck yesterday, so I guess it will hold my car today. That bridge ought to stand for a while yet." Briefly she wondered whether she might not say "for a spell" instead of "for a while," and then decided that sooner or later it would come naturally. "Anyway, who minds rain? We've got so much to do indoors." She was pleased with "indoors."

"Well," the clerk said, "of course, no one can stop you from driving on the old Sanderson road. If you want to. You'll find people around here mostly leave it alone in the rain, though. Myself, I think it's all just gossip, but then, I don't drive out that way much, anyway."

"It's a little muddy on a day like this," Ethel Sloane said firmly, "and maybe a little scary crossing the bridge when the creek is high, but you've got to expect that kind of thing when you live in the country."

"I wasn't talking about that," the clerk said. "Closet hooks? I wonder, do we have any closet hooks."

In the grocery Ethel Sloane bought mustard and soap and pickles and flour. "All the things I forgot to get yesterday," she explained, laughing.

"You took that road on a day like this?" the grocer asked.

"It's not that bad," she said, surprised again. "I don't mind the rain."

"We don't use that road in this weather," the grocer said. "You might say there's talk about that road."

"It certainly seems to have quite a local reputation," Ethel said, and laughed. "And it's nowhere near as bad as some of the other roads I've seen around here."

"Well, I told you," the grocer said, and shut his mouth.

I've offended him, Ethel thought, I've said I think their roads are bad; these people are so jealous of their countryside.

"I guess our road is pretty muddy," she said almost apologetically. "But I'm really a very careful driver."

"You stay careful," the grocer said. "No matter what you see."

"I'm always careful." Whistling, Ethel Sloane went out and got into her car and turned in the circle in front of the abandoned railway station. Nice little town, she was thinking, and they are beginning to like us already, all so worried about my safe driving. We're the kind of people, Jim and I, who fit in a place like this; we wouldn't belong in the suburbs or some kind of a colony; we're real people. Jim will write, she thought, and I'll get one of these country women to teach me how to make bread. Watson for plumbing.

She was oddly touched when the clerk from the hardware store and then the grocer stepped to their doorways to watch her drive by. They're worrying about me, she thought; they're afraid a city gal can't manage their bad, wicked roads, and I do bet it's hell in the winter, but I can manage; I'm country now.

Her way led out of the village and then off the highway onto a dirt road that meandered between fields and an occasional farmhouse, then crossed the creek—disturbingly high after all this rain—and turned onto the steep hill that led to the Sanderson house. Ethel Sloane could see the house from the bridge across the creek, although in summer the view would be hidden by trees. It's a lovely house, she thought with a little catch of pride; I'm so lucky; up there it stands, so proud and remote, waiting for me to come home.

On one side of the hill the Sanderson land had long ago been sold off, and the hillside was dotted with small cottages and a couple of ramshackle farms; the people on that side of the hill used the other, lower, road, and Ethel Sloane was surprised and a little uneasy to perceive that the tire marks on this road and across the bridge were all her own, coming down; no one else seemed to use this road at all. Private, anyway, she thought; maybe they've talked everyone else out of using it. She looked up to see the house as she crossed the bridge; my very own house, she thought, and then, well, *our* very own house, she thought, and then she saw that there were two figures standing silently in the rain by the side of the road.

Good heavens, she thought, standing there in this rain, and she stopped the car. "Can I give you a lift?" she called out, rolling down the window. Through the rain she could see that they seemed to be an old woman and a child, and the rain drove down on them. Staring, Ethel Sloane became aware that the child was sick with misery, wet and shivering and crying in the rain, and she said sharply, "Come and get in the car at once; you mustn't keep that child out in the rain another minute."

They stared at her, the old woman frowning, listening. Perhaps she is deaf, Ethel thought, and in her good raincoat and solid boots she climbed out of the car and went over to them. Not wanting for any reason in the world to touch either of them, she put her face close to the old woman's and said urgently, "Come, hurry. Get that child into the car, where it's dry. I'll take you wherever you want to go." Then, with real horror, she saw that the child was wrapped in a blanket, and under the blanket he was wearing thin pajamas; with a shiver of fury, Ethel saw that he was barefoot and standing in the mud. "Get in that car at once," she said, and hurried to open the back door. "Get in that car at once, do you hear me?"

Silently the old woman reached her hand down to the child and, his eyes wide and staring past Ethel Sloane, the child moved toward the car, with the old woman following. Ethel looked in disgust at the small bare feet going over the mud and rocks, and she said to the old woman, "You ought to be ashamed; that child is certainly going to be sick."

She waited until they had climbed into the backseat of the car, and then slammed the door and got into her seat again. She glanced up at the mirror, but they were sitting in the corner, where she could not see them, and she turned; the child was huddled against the old woman, and the old woman looked straight ahead, her face heavy with weariness.

"Where are you going?" Ethel asked, her voice rising. "Where shall I take you? That child," she said to the old woman, "has to be gotten indoors and into dry clothes as soon as possible. Where are you going? I'll see that you get there in a hurry."

The old woman opened her mouth, and in a voice of old age beyond consolation said, "We want to go to the Sanderson place."

"To the Sanderson place?" To us? Ethel thought, To see us? This pair? Then she realized that the Sanderson place, to the old local people, probably still included the land where the cottages had been built; they probably still call the whole thing the Sanderson place, she thought, and felt oddly feudal with pride. Were the lords of the manor, she thought, and her voice was more gentle when she asked, "Were you waiting out there for very long in the rain?"

"Yes," the old woman said, her voice remote and despairing. Their lives must be desolate, Ethel thought. Imagine being that old and that tired and standing in the rain for someone to come by.

"Well, we'll soon have you home," she said, and started the car. The wheels slipped and skidded in the mud, but found a purchase, and slowly Ethel felt the car begin to move up the hill. It was very muddy, and the rain was heavier, and the back of the car dragged as though under an intolerable weight. It's as though I had a load of iron, Ethel thought. Poor old lady, it's the weight of years.

"Is the child all right?" she asked, lifting her head; she could not turn to look at them.

"He wants to go home," the old woman said.

"I should think so. Tell him it won't be long. I'll take you right to your door," It's the least I can do, she thought, and maybe go inside with them and see that he's warm enough; those poor bare feet.

Driving up the hill was very difficult, and perhaps the road was a little worse than Ethel had believed; she found that she could not look around or even speak while she was navigating the sharp curves, with the rain driving against the windshield and the wheels slipping in the mud. Once she said, "Nearly at the top," and then had to be silent, holding the wheel tight. When the car gave a final lurch and topped the small last rise that led onto the flat driveway before the Sanderson house, Ethel said, "Made it," and laughed. "Now, which way should I go?"

They're frightened, she thought. I'm sure the child is frightened and I don't blame them; I was a little nervous myself. She said loudly, "We're at the top now, it's all right, we made it. Now where shall I take you?"

When there was still no answer, she turned; the backseat of the car was empty.

"But even if they *could* have gotten out of the car without my noticing," Ethel Sloane said for the tenth time that evening to her husband, "they couldn't have gotten out of sight. I looked and looked." She lifted her hands in an emphatic gesture. "I went all around the top of the hill in the rain looking in all directions and calling them."

"But the car seat was dry," her husband said.

"Well, you're not going to suggest that I imagined it, are you? Because I'm simply not the kind of *person* to dream up an old lady and a sick child. There has to be some *explanation*; I don't imagine things."

"Well..." Jim said, and hesitated.

"Are you sure you didn't see them? They didn't come to the door?"

"Listen..." Jim said, and hesitated again. "Look," he said.

"I have certainly *never* been the kind of person who goes around imagining that she sees old ladies and children. You know me better than that, Jim, you know I don't go around—"

"Well," Jim said. "Look," he said finally, "there *could* be something. A story I heard. I never told you because—"

"Because what?"

"Because you... well—" Jim said.

"Jim." Ethel Sloane set her lips. "I don't like this,

Jim. What is there that you haven't told me? Is there really something you know and I don't?"

"It's just a story. I heard it when I came up to look at the house."

"Do you mean you've known something all this time and you've never told me?"

"It's just a story," Jim said helplessly. Then, looking away, he said, "Everyone knows it, but they don't say much, I mean, these things—"

"Jim," Ethel said, "tell me at once."

"It's just that there was a little Sanderson boy stolen or lost or something. They thought a crazy old woman took him. People kept talking about it, but they never knew anything for sure."

"What?" Ethel Sloane stood up and started for the door. "You mean there's a child been stolen and no one told me about it?"

"No," Jim said oddly. "I mean, it happened sixty years ago."

Ethel was still talking about it at breakfast the next morning. "And they've never been found," she told herself happily. "All the people around went searching, and they finally decided the two of them had drowned in the creek, because it was raining then just the way it is now." She glanced with satisfaction at the rain beating against the window of the breakfast room. "Oh, lovely," she said, and sighed, and stretched, and smiled. "Ghosts," she said. "I saw two honest-to-goodness ghosts. No wonder," she said, "no *wonder* the child looked so awful. Awful! Kidnapped, and then drowned. No *wonder*."

"Listen," Jim said, "if I were you, I'd forget about it. People around here don't like to talk much about it."

"They wouldn't tell me," Ethel said, and laughed again. "Our very own ghosts, and not a soul would tell me. I just won't be satisfied until I get every word of the story."

"That's why *I* never told you," Jim said miserably.

"Don't be silly. Yesterday everyone I spoke to mentioned my driving on that road, and I bet every one of them was dying to tell me the story. I can't wait to see their faces when they hear."

"No." Jim stared at her. "You simply *can't* go around… *boasting* about it."

"But of course I can! Now we really belong here. I've really seen the local ghosts. And I'm going in this morning and tell everybody, and find out all I can."

"I wish you wouldn't," Jim said.

"I know you wish I wouldn't, but I'm going to. If I listened to you, I'd wait and wait for a good time to mention it and maybe even come to believe I'd dreamed it or something, so I'm going into the village right after breakfast."

"Please, Ethel," Jim said. "Please listen to me. People might not take it the way you think."

"Two ghosts of our very own." Ethel laughed again. "My very own," she said. "I just can't wait to see their faces in the village."

Before she got into the car she opened the back door and looked again at the seat, dry and unmarked. Then, smiling to herself, she got into the driver's seat and, suddenly touched with sick cold, turned around to look. "Why," she said, half whispering, "you're not *still* here, you can't be! Why," she said, "I just looked."

"They were strangers in the house," the old woman said.

The skin on the back of Ethel's neck crawled as though some wet thing walked there; the child stared past her, and the old woman's eyes were flat and dead. "What do you want?" Ethel asked, still whispering.

"We got to go back."

"I'll take you." The rain came hard against the windows of the car, and Ethel Sloane, seeing her own hand tremble as she reached for the car key, told herself, don't be afraid, don't be afraid, they're not real. "I'll take you," she said, gripping the wheel tight and turning the car to face down the hill, "I'll take you," she said, almost babbling, "I'll take you right back, I promise, see if I don't, I promise I'll take you right back where you want to go."

"He wanted to go home," the old woman said. Her voice was very far away.

"I'll take you, I'll take you." The road was even more slippery than before, and Ethel Sloane told herself, drive carefully, don't be afraid, they're not real. "Right where I found you yesterday, the very spot, I'll take you back."

"They were strangers in the house."

Ethel realized that she was driving faster than she should; she felt the disgusting wet cold coming from the backseat pushing her, forcing her to hurry.

"I'll take you back," she said over and over to the old woman and the child.

"When the strangers are gone, we can go home," the old woman said.

Coming to the last turn before the bridge, the wheels slipped, and, pulling at the steering wheel and shouting, "I'll take you back, I'll take you back," Ethel Sloane could hear only the child's horrible laughter as the car turned and skidded toward the high waters of the creek. One wheel slipped and spun in the air, and then, wrenching at the car with all her strength, she pulled it back onto the road and stopped.

Crying, breathless, Ethel put her head down on the steering wheel, weak and exhausted. I was almost killed, she told herself, they almost took me with them. She did not need to look into the backseat of the car; the cold was gone, and she knew the seat was dry and empty.

The clerk in the hardware store looked up and, seeing Ethel Sloane, smiled politely and then, looking again, frowned. "You feeling poorly this morning, Mrs Sloane?" he asked. "Rain bothering you?"

"I almost had an accident on the road," Ethel Sloane said.

"On the old Sanderson road?" The clerk's hands were very still on the counter. "An accident?"

Ethel Sloane opened her mouth and then shut it again. "Yes," she said at last. "The car skidded."

"We don't use that road much," the clerk said. Ethel started to speak, but stopped herself.

"It's got a bad name locally, that road," he said. "What were you needing this morning?"

Ethel thought, and finally said, "Clothespins, I guess I must need clothespins. About the Sanderson road—"

"Yes?" said the clerk, his back to her.

"Nothing," Ethel said.

"Clothespins," the clerk said, putting a box on the counter. "By the way, will you and the mister be coming to the P.T.A. social tomorrow night?"

"We certainly will," said Ethel Sloane.

A GHOST STORY

Mark Twain

I TOOK A LARGE ROOM, far up Broadway, in a huge old building whose upper stories had been wholly unoccupied for years until I came. The place had long been given up to dust and cobwebs, to solitude and silence. I seemed groping among the tombs and invading the privacy of the dead, that first night I climbed up to my quarters. For the first time in my life a superstitious dread came over me; and as I turned a dark angle of the stairway and an invisible cobweb swung its slazy woof in my face and clung there, I shuddered as one who had encountered a phantom.

I was glad enough when I reached my room and locked out the mold and the darkness. A cheery fire was burning in the grate, and I sat down before it with a comforting sense of relief. For two hours I sat there, thinking of bygone times; recalling old scenes, and summoning half-forgotten faces out of the mists of the past; listening, in fancy, to voices that long ago grew silent for all time, and to once familiar songs that nobody sings now. And as my reverie softened down to a sadder and sadder pathos, the shrieking of the winds outside softened to a wail, the angry beating of the rain against the panes diminished to a tranquil patter, and one by one the noises in the street subsided, until the hurrying footsteps of the last belated straggler died away in the distance and left no sound behind.

The fire had burned low. A sense of loneliness crept over me. I arose and undressed, moving on tiptoe about the room, doing stealthily what I had to do, as if I were environed by sleeping enemies whose slumbers it would be fatal to break. I covered up in bed, and lay listening to the rain and wind and the faint creaking of distant shutters, till they lulled me to sleep.

I slept profoundly, but how long I do not know. All at once I found myself awake, and filled with a shuddering expectancy. All was still. All but my own heart—I could hear it beat. Presently the bedclothes began to slip away slowly toward the foot of the bed, as if someone were pulling them! I could not stir; I could not speak. Still the blankets slipped deliberately away, till my breast was uncovered. Then with a great effort I seized them and drew them over my head. I waited, listened, waited. Once more that steady pull began, and once more I lay torpid a century of dragging seconds till my breast was naked again. At last I roused my energies and snatched the covers back to their place and held them with a strong grip. I waited. By and by I felt a faint tug, and took a fresh grip. The tug strengthened to a steady strain—it grew stronger and stronger. My hold parted, and for the third time the blankets slid away. I groaned. An answering groan came from the foot of the bed! Beaded drops of sweat stood upon my forehead. I was more dead than alive. Presently I heard a heavy footstep in my room—the step of an elephant, it seemed to me—it was not like anything human. But it was moving from me—there was relief in that. I heard it approach the door—pass out without moving bolt or lock—and wander away among the dismal corridors, straining the floors and joists till they creaked again as it passed—and then silence reigned once more.

When my excitement had calmed, I said to myself, "This is a dream—simply a hideous dream." And so

I lay thinking it over until I convinced myself that it was a dream, and then a comforting laugh relaxed my lips and I was happy again. I got up and struck a light; and when I found that the locks and bolts were just as I had left them, another soothing laugh welled in my heart and rippled from my lips. I took my pipe and lit it, and was just sitting down before the fire, when—down went the pipe out of my nerveless fingers, the blood forsook my cheeks, and my placid breathing was cut short with a gasp! In the ashes on the hearth, side by side with my own bare footprint, was another, so vast that in comparison mine was but an infant's! Then I *had* had a visitor, and the elephant tread was explained.

I put out the light and returned to bed, palsied with fear. I lay a long time, peering into the darkness, and listening. Then I heard a grating noise overhead, like the dragging of a heavy body across the floor; then the throwing down of the body, and the shaking of my windows in response to the concussion. In distant parts of the building I heard the muffled slamming of doors. I heard, at intervals, stealthy footsteps creeping in and out among the corridors, and up and down the stairs. Sometimes these noises approached my door, hesitated, and went away again. I heard the clanking of chains faintly, in remote passages, and listened while the clanking grew nearer—while it wearily climbed the stairways, marking each move by the loose surplus of chain that fell with an accented rattle upon each succeeding step as the goblin that bore it advanced. I heard muttered sentences; half-uttered screams that seemed smothered violently; and the swish of invisible garments, the rush of invisible wings. Then I became conscious that my chamber was invaded—that I was not alone. I heard sighs and breathings about my bed, and mysterious whisperings. Three little spheres of soft phosphorescent light appeared on the ceiling directly over my head, clung and glowed there a moment, and then dropped—two of them upon my face and one upon the pillow. They spattered, liquidly, and felt warm. Intuition told me they had turned to gouts of blood as they fell—I needed no light to satisfy myself of that. Then I saw pallid faces, dimly luminous, and white uplifted hands, floating bodiless in the air—floating a moment and then disappearing. The whispering ceased, and the voices and the sounds, and a solemn stillness followed. I waited and listened. I felt that I must have light or die. I was weak with fear. I slowly raised myself toward a sitting posture, and my face came in contact with a clammy hand! All strength went from me apparently, and I fell back like a stricken invalid. Then I heard the rustle of a garment—it seemed to pass to the door and go out.

When everything was still once more, I crept out of bed, sick and feeble, and lit the gas with a hand that trembled as if it were aged with a hundred years. The light brought some little cheer to my spirits. I sat down and fell into a dreamy contemplation of that great footprint in the ashes. By and by its outlines began to waver and grow dim. I glanced up and the broad gas flame was slowly wilting away. In the same moment I heard that elephantine tread again. I noted its approach, nearer and nearer, along the musty halls, and dimmer and dimmer the light waned. The tread reached my very door and paused—the light had dwindled to a sickly blue, and all things about me lay in a spectral twilight. The door did not open, and yet I felt a faint gust of air fan my cheek, and presently was conscious of a huge, cloudy presence before me. I watched it with fascinated eyes. A pale glow stole over the Thing; gradually its cloudy folds took shape—an arm appeared, then legs, then a body, and last a great sad face looked out of the vapor. Stripped of its filmy housings, naked, muscular and comely, the majestic Cardiff Giant loomed above me!

All my misery vanished—for a child might know that no harm could come with that benignant countenance. My cheerful spirits returned at once, and in sympathy with them the gas flamed up brightly again. Never a lonely outcast was so glad to welcome company as I was to greet the friendly giant. I said:

"Why, is it nobody but you? Do you know, I have been scared to death for the last two or three hours? I am most honestly glad to see you. I wish I had a chair—Here, here, don't try to sit down in that thing—"

But it was too late. He was in it before I could stop him and down he went—I never saw a chair shivered so in my life.

"Stop, stop, you'll ruin ev—"

Too late again. There was another crash, and another chair was resolved into its original elements.

"Confound it, haven't you got any judgment at all? Do you want to ruin all the furniture on the place? Here, here, you petrified fool—"

But it was no use. Before I could arrest him he had sat down on the bed, and it was a melancholy ruin.

"Now what sort of a way is that to do? First you come lumbering about the place bringing a legion of vagabond goblins along with you to worry me to death, and then when I overlook an indelicacy of costume which would not be tolerated anywhere by cultivated people except in a respectable theater, and not even there if the nudity were of your sex, you repay me by wrecking all the furniture you can find to sit down on. And why will you? You damage yourself as much as you do me. You have broken off the end of your spinal column, and littered up the floor with chips of your hams till the place looks like a marble yard. You ought to be ashamed of yourself—you are big enough to know better."

"Well, I will not break any more furniture. But what am I to do? I have not had a chance to sit down for a century." And the tears came into his eyes.

"Poor devil," I said, "I should not have been so harsh with you. And you are an orphan, too, no doubt. But sit down on the floor here—nothing else can stand your weight—and besides, we cannot be sociable with you away up there above me; I want you down where I can perch on this high counting-house stool and gossip with you face to face."

So he sat down on the floor, and lit a pipe which I gave him, threw one of my red blankets over his shoulders, inverted my sitz bath on his head, helmet fashion, and made himself picturesque and comfortable. Then he crossed his ankles, while I renewed the fire, and exposed the flat, honeycombed bottoms of his prodigious feet to the grateful warmth.

"What is the matter with the bottom of your feet and the back of your legs, that they are gouged up so?"

"Infernal chilblains—I caught them clear up to the back of my head, roosting out there under Newell's farm. But I love the place; I love it as one loves his old home. There is no peace for me like the peace I feel when I am there."

We talked along for half an hour, and then I noticed that he looked tired, and spoke of it.

"Tired?" he said. "Well, I should think so. And now I will tell you all about it, since you have treated me so well. I am the spirit of the Petrified Man that lies across the street there in the museum. I am the ghost of the Cardiff Giant. I can have no rest, no peace, till they have given that poor body burial again. Now what was the most natural thing for me to do, to make men satisfy this wish? Terrify them into it!—haunt the place where the body lay! So I haunted the museum night after night. I even got other spirits to help me. But it did no good, for nobody ever came to the museum at midnight. Then it occurred to me to come over the way and haunt this place a little. I felt that if I ever got a hearing I must succeed, for I had the most efficient company that perdition could furnish. Night after night we have shivered around through these mildewed halls, dragging chains, groaning, whispering, tramping up and down stairs, till, to tell you the truth, I am almost worn out. But when I saw a light in your room tonight I roused my energies again and went at it with a deal of the old freshness. But I am tired out—entirely fagged out. Give me, I beseech you, give me some hope!"

I lit off my perch in a burst of excitement, and exclaimed:

"This transcends everything! everything that ever did occur! Why you poor blundering old fossil, you have had all your trouble for nothing—you have been haunting a plaster cast of yourself—the real Cardiff Giant is in Albany!—[A fact. The original fraud was ingeniously and fraudfully duplicated, and exhibited in New York as the "only genuine" Cardiff Giant (to the unspeakable disgust of the owners of the real colossus) at the very same time that the latter was drawing crowds at a museum in Albany]—Confound it, don't you know your own remains?"

I never saw such an eloquent look of shame, of pitiable humiliation, overspread a countenance before.

The Petrified Man rose slowly to his feet, and said:

"Honestly, is that true?"

"As true as I am sitting here."

He took the pipe from his mouth and laid it on the mantel, then stood irresolute a moment (unconsciously, from old habit, thrusting his hands where his pantaloons pockets should have been, and meditatively dropping his chin on his breast) and finally said:

"Well—I never felt so absurd before. The Petrified Man has sold everybody else, and now the mean fraud has ended by selling its own ghost! My son, if there is any charity left in your heart for a poor friendless phantom like me, don't let this get out. Think how you would feel if you had made such an ass of yourself."

I heard his stately tramp die away, step by step down the stairs and out into the deserted street, and felt sorry that he was gone, poor fellow—and sorrier still that he had carried off my red blanket and my bathtub.

SPUNK

Zora Neale Hurston

I

A GIANT of a brown-skinned man sauntered up the one street of the Village and out into the palmetto thickets with a small pretty woman clinging lovingly to his arm.

"Looka theah, folkses!" cried Elijah Mosley, slapping his leg gleefully. "Theah they go, big as life an' brassy as tacks."

All the loungers in the store tried to walk to the door with an air of nonchalance but with small success.

"Now pee-eople!" Walter Thomas gasped. "Will you look at 'em!"

"But that's one thing Ah likes about Spunk Banks—he ain't skeered of nothin' on God's green footstool—nothin'! He rides that log down at sawmill jus' like he struts 'round wid another man's wife—jus' don't give a kitty. When Tes' Miller got cut to giblets on that circle saw, Spunk steps right up and starts ridin'. The rest of us was skeered to go near it."

A round-shouldered figure in overalls much too large, came nervously in the door and the talking ceased. The men looked at each other and winked.

"Gimme some soda water. Sass'prilla Ah reckon," the newcomer ordered, and stood far down the counter near the open pickled pig-feet tub to drink it.

Elijah nudged Walter and turned with mock gravity to the newcomer.

"Say, Joe, how's everything up yo' way? How's yo' wife?"

Joe started and all but dropped the bottle he held in his hands. He swallowed several times painfully and his lips trembled.

"Aw 'Lige, you oughtn't to do nothin' like that," Walter grumbled. Elijah ignored him.

"She jus' passed heah a few minutes ago goin' theta way," with a wave of his hand in the direction of the woods.

Now Joe knew his wife had passed that way. He knew that the men lounging in the general store had seen her, moreover, he knew that the men knew he knew. He stood there silent for a long moment staring blankly, with his Adam's apple twitching nervously up and down his throat. One could actually see the pain he was suffering, his eyes, his face, his hands and even the dejected slump of his shoulders. He set the bottle down upon the counter. He didn't bang it, just eased it out of his hand silently and fiddled with his suspender buckle.

"Well, Ah'm goin' after her today. Ah'm goin' an' fetch her back. Spunk's done gone too fur."

He reached deep down into his trouser pocket and drew out a hollow ground razor, large and shiny, and passed his moistened thumb back and forth over the edge.

"Talkin' like a man, Joe. Course that's yo' fambly affairs, but Ah like to see grit in anybody."

Joe Kanty laid down a nickel and stumbled out into the street.

Dusk crept in from the woods. Ike Clarke lit the swinging oil lamp that was almost immediately surrounded by candle flies. The men laughed boisterously behind Joe's back as they watched him shamble woodward.

"You oughtn't to said whut you did to him, 'Lige—look how it worked him up," Walter chided.

"And Ah hope it did work him up. 'Tain't even decent for a man to take and take like he do."

"Spunk will sho' kill him."

"Aw, Ah doan't know. You never kin tell. He might turn him up an' spank him fur gettin' in the way, but Spunk wouldn't shoot no unarmed man. Dat razor he carried outa heah ain't gonna run Spunk down an' cut him, an' Joe ain't got the nerve to go up to Spunk with it knowing he totes that Army 45. He makes that break outa heah to bluff us. He's gonna hide that razor behind the first likely palmetto root an' sneak back home to bed. Don't tell me nothin' 'bout that rabbit-foot colored man. Didn't he meet Spunk an' Lena face to face one day las' week an' mumble sumthin' to Spunk 'bout lettin' his wife alone?"

"What did Spunk say?" Walter broke in—"Ah like him fine but 'tain't right the way he carries on wid Lena Kanty, jus' cause Joe's timid 'bout fightin'."

"You wrong theah, Walter. 'Tain't cause Joe's timid at all, it's cause Spunk wants Lena. If Joe was a passle of wile cats Spunk would tackle the job just the same. He'd go after anything he wanted the same way. As Ah wuz sayin' a minute ago, he tole Joe right to his face that Lena was his. 'Call her,' he says to Joe. 'Call her and see if she'll come. A woman knows her boss an' she answers when he calls.' 'Lena, ain't I yo' husband?' Joe sorter whines out. Lena looked at him real disgusted but she don't answer and she don't move outa her tracks. Then Spunk reaches out an' takes hold of her arm an' says: 'Lena, youse mine. From now on Ah works for you an' fights for you an' Ah never wants you to look to nobody for a crumb of bread, a stitch of close or a shingle to go over yo' head, but me long as Ah live. Ah'll git the lumber foh owah house tomorrow. Go home an' git yo' things together!'

"'Thass mah house,' Lena speaks up. 'Papa gimme that.'

"'Well,' says Spunk, 'doan give up whut's yours, but when youse inside don't forgit youse mine, an' let no other man git outa his place wid you!'

"Lena looked up at him with her eyes so full of love that they wuz runnin' over, an' Spunk seen it an' Joe seen it too, and his lip started to tremblin' and his Adam's apple was galloping up and down his neck like a racehorse. Ah bet he's wore out half a dozen Adam's apples since Spunk's been on the job with Lena. That's all he'll do. He'll be back heah after while swallowin' an' workin' his lips like he wants to say somethin' an' can't."

"But didn't he do nothin' to stop 'em?"

"Nope, not a frazzlin' thing—jus' stood there. Spunk took Lena's arm and walked off jus' like nothin' ain't happened and he stood there gazin' after them till they was outa sight. Now you know a woman don't want no man like that. I'm jus' waitin' to see whut he's goin' to say when he gits back."

II

But Joe Kanty never came back, never. The men in the store heard the sharp report of a pistol somewhere distant in the palmetto thicket and soon Spunk came walking leisurely, with his big black Stetson set at the same rakish angle and Lena clinging to his arm, came walking right into the general store. Lena wept in a frightened manner.

"Well," Spunk announced calmly, "Joe come out there wid a meatax an' made me kill him."

He sent Lena home and led the men back to Joe—Joe crumpled and limp with his right hand still clutching his razor.

"See mah back? Mah cloes cut clear through. He sneaked up an' tried to kill me from the back, but

Ah got him, an' got him good, first shot," Spunk said.

The men glared at Elijah, accusingly.

"Take him up an' plant him in 'Stoney lonesome,"' Spunk said in a careless voice. "Ah didn't wanna shoot him but he made me do it. He's a dirty coward, jumpin' on a man from behind."

Spunk turned on his heel and sauntered away to where he knew his love wept in fear for him and no man stopped him. At the general store later on, they all talked of locking him up until the sheriff should come from Orlando, but no one did anything but talk.

A clear case of self-defense, the trial was a short one, and Spunk walked out of the courthouse to freedom again. He could work again, ride the dangerous log-carriage that fed the singing, snarling, biting, circle saw; he could stroll the soft dark lanes with his guitar. He was free to roam the woods again; he was free to return to Lena. He did all of these things.

III

"Whut you reckon, Walt?" Elijah asked one night later. "Spunk's gittin' ready to marry Lena!"

"Naw! Why, Joe ain't had time to git cold yit. Nohow Ah didn't figger Spunk was the marryin' kind."

"Well, he is," rejoined Elijah. "He done moved most of Lena's things—and her along wid 'em—over to the Bradley house. He's buying it. Jus' like Ah told yo' all right in heah the night Joe wuz kilt. Spunk's crazy 'bout Lena. He don't want folks to keep on talkin' 'bout her—thass reason he's rushin' so. Funny thing 'bout that bobcat, wan't it?"

"What bobcat, 'Lige? Ah ain't heered 'bout none."

"Ain't cher? Well, night befo' las' was the fust night Spunk an' Lena moved together an' jus' as they was goin' to bed, a big black bobcat, black all over, you hear me, black, walked round and round that house and howled like forty, an' when Spunk got his gun an' went to the winder to shoot it he says it stood right still an' looked him in the eye, an' howled right at him. The thing got Spunk so nervoused up he couldn't shoot. But Spunk says twan't no bobcat nohow. He says it was Joe done sneaked back from Hell!"

"Humph!" sniffed Walter, "he oughter be nervous after what he done. Ah reckon Joe come back to dare him to marry Lena, or to come out an' fight. Ah bet he'll be back time and agin, too. Know what Ah think? Joe wuz a braver man than Spunk."

There was a general shout of derision from the group.

"Thass a fact," went on Walter. "Lookit whut he done took a razor an' went out to fight a man he knowed toted a gun an' wuz a crack shot, too; 'nother thing Joe wuz skeered of Spunk, skeered plumb stiff! But he went jes' the same. It took him a long time to get his nerve up. 'Tain't nothin' for Spunk to fight when he ain't skeered of nothin'. Now, Joe's done come back to have it out wid the man that's got all he ever had. Y'll know Joe ain't never had nothin' nor wanted nothin' besides Lena. It musta been a h'ant cause ain' nobody never seen no black bobcat."

"'Nother thing," cut in one of the men, "Spunk wuz cussin' a blue streak today 'cause he 'lowed dat saw wuz wobblin'—almos' got 'im once. The machinist come, looked it over an' said it wuz alright. Spunk musta been leanin' t'wards it some. Den he claimed somebody pushed 'im but 'twant nobody close to 'im. Ah wuz glad when knockin' off time come. I'm skeered of dat man when he gits hot. He'd beat you full of buttonholes as quick as he's look etcher."

IV

The men gathered the next evening in a different mood, no laughter. No badinage this time.

"Look, 'Lige, you goin' to set up wid Spunk?"

"Naw, Ah reckon not, Walter. Tell yuh the truth, Ah'm a lil bit skittish. Spunk died too wicket—died cussin' he did. You know he thought he wuz done outa life."

"Good Lawd, who'd he think done it?"

"Joe."

"Joe Kanty? How come?"

"Walter, Ah b'leeve Ah will walk up theta way an' set. Lena would like it Ah reckon."

"But whut did he say, 'Lige?"

Elijah did not answer until they had left the lighted store and were strolling down the dark street.

"Ah wuz loadin' a wagon wid scantlin' right near the saw when Spunk fell on the carriage but 'fore Ah could git to him the saw got him in the body—awful sight. Me an' Skint Miller got him off but it was too late. Anybody could see that. The fust thing he said wuz: 'He pushed me, 'Lige—the dirty hound pushed me in the back!'—He was spittin' blood at ev'ry breath. We laid him on the sawdust pile with his face to the East so's he could die easy. He heft mah hen' till the last, Walter, and said: 'It was Joe, 'Lige—the dirty sneak shoved me... he didn't dare come to mah face... but Ah'll git the son-of-a-woodlouse soon's Ah get there an' make hell too hot for him... Ah felt him shove me!...' Thass how he died."

"If spirits kin fight, there's a powerful tussle goin' on somewhere ovah Jordan 'cause Ah b'leeve Joe's ready for Spunk an' ain't skeered any more—yes, Ah b'leeve Joe pushed 'im mahself."

They had arrived at the house. Lena's lamentations were deep and loud. She had filled the room with magnolia blossoms that gave off a heavy sweet odor. The keepers of the wake tipped about whispering in frightened tones. Everyone in the village was there, even old Jeff Kanty, Joe's father, who a few hours before would have been afraid to come within ten feet of him, stood leering triumphantly down upon the fallen giant as if his fingers had been the teeth of steel that laid him low.

The cooling board consisted of three sixteen-inch boards on saw horses, a dingy sheet was his shroud.

The women ate heartily of the funeral baked meats and wondered who would be Lena's next. The men whispered coarse conjectures between guzzles of whiskey.

THE YELLOW WALLPAPER

Charlotte Perkins Gilman

IT IS VERY SELDOM that mere ordinary people like John and myself secure ancestral halls for the summer.

A colonial mansion, a hereditary estate, I would say a haunted house, and reach the height of romantic felicity—but that would be asking too much of fate!

Still I will proudly declare that there is something queer about it.

Else, why should it be let so cheaply? And why have stood so long untenanted?

John laughs at me, of course, but one expects that in marriage.

John is practical in the extreme. He has no patience with faith, an intense horror of superstition, and he scoffs openly at any talk of things not to be felt and seen and put down in figures.

John is a physician, and *perhaps*—(I would not say it to a living soul, of course, but this is dead paper and a great relief to my mind)—*perhaps* that is one reason I do not get well faster.

You see, he does not believe I am sick!

And what can one do?

If a physician of high standing, and one's own husband, assures friends and relatives that there is really nothing the matter with one but temporary nervous depression—a slight hysterical tendency—what is one to do?

My brother is also a physician, and also of high standing, and he says the same thing.

So I take phosphates or phosphites—whichever it is, and tonics, and journeys, and air, and exercise, and am absolutely forbidden to "work" until I am well again.

Personally, I disagree with their ideas.

Personally, I believe that congenial work, with excitement and change, would do me good.

But what is one to do?

I did write for a while in spite of them; but it *does* exhaust me a good deal—having to be so sly about it, or else meet with heavy opposition.

I sometimes fancy that in my condition if I had

less opposition and more society and stimulus—but John says the very worst thing I can do is to think about my condition, and I confess it always makes me feel bad.

So I will let it alone and talk about the house.

The most beautiful place! It is quite alone, standing well back from the road, quite three miles from the village. It makes me think of English places that you read about, for there are hedges and walls and gates that lock, and lots of separate little houses for the gardeners and people.

There is a *delicious* garden! I never saw such a garden—large and shady, full of box-bordered paths, and lined with long grape-covered arbors with seats under them.

There were greenhouses, too, but they are all broken now.

There was some legal trouble, I believe, something about the heirs and co-heirs; anyhow, the place has been empty for years.

That spoils my ghostliness, I am afraid; but I don't care—there is something strange about the house—I can feel it.

I even said so to John one moonlight evening, but he said what I felt was a *draught*, and shut the window.

I get unreasonably angry with John sometimes. I'm sure I never used to be so sensitive. I think it is due to this nervous condition.

But John says if I feel so I shall neglect proper self-control; so I take pains to control myself—before him, at least—and that makes me very tired.

I don't like our room a bit. I wanted one downstairs that opened on the piazza and had roses all over the window, and such pretty old-fashioned chintz hangings! but John would not hear of it.

He said there was only one window and not room for two beds, and no near room for him if he took another.

He is very careful and loving, and hardly lets me stir without special direction.

I have a schedule prescription for each hour in the day; he takes all care from me, and so I feel basely ungrateful not to value it more.

He said we came here solely on my account, that I was to have perfect rest and all the air I could get. "Your exercise depends on your strength, my dear," said he, "and your food somewhat on your appetite; but air you can absorb all the time." So we took the nursery, at the top of the house.

It is a big, airy room, the whole floor nearly, with windows that look all ways, and air and sunshine galore. It was nursery first and then playground and gymnasium, I should judge; for the windows are barred for little children, and there are rings and things in the walls.

The paint and paper look as if a boys' school had used it. It is stripped off—the paper—in great patches all around the head of my bed, about as far as I can reach, and in a great place on the other side of the room low down. I never saw a worse paper in my life.

One of those sprawling flamboyant patterns committing every artistic sin.

It is dull enough to confuse the eye in following, pronounced enough to constantly irritate, and provoke study, and when you follow the lame, uncertain curves for a little distance they suddenly commit suicide—plunge off at outrageous angles, destroy themselves in unheard-of contradictions.

The color is repellant, almost revolting; a smouldering, unclean yellow, strangely faded by the slow-turning sunlight.

It is a dull yet lurid orange in some places, a sickly sulphur tint in others.

No wonder the children hated it! I should hate it myself if I had to live in this room long.

There comes John, and I must put this away—he hates to have me write a word.

We have been here two weeks, and I haven't felt like writing before, since that first day.

I am sitting by the window now, up in this atrocious nursery, and there is nothing to hinder my writing as much as I please, save lack of strength.

John is away all day, and even some nights when his cases are serious.

I am glad my case is not serious!

But these nervous troubles are dreadfully depressing.

John does not know how much I really suffer. He knows there is no *reason* to suffer, and that satisfies him.

Of course it is only nervousness. It does weigh on me so not to do my duty in any way!

I meant to be such a help to John, such a real rest and comfort, and here I am a comparative burden already!

Nobody would believe what an effort it is to do what little I am able—to dress and entertain, and order things.

It is fortunate Mary is so good with the baby. Such a dear baby!

And yet I *cannot* be with him, it makes me so nervous.

I suppose John never was nervous in his life. He laughs at me so about this wallpaper!

At first he meant to repaper the room, but afterwards he said that I was letting it get the better of me, and that nothing was worse for a nervous patient than to give way to such fancies.

He said that after the wallpaper was changed it would be the heavy bedstead, and then the barred windows, and then that gate at the head of the stairs, and so on.

"You know the place is doing you good," he said, "and really, dear, I don't care to renovate the house just for a three months' rental."

"Then do let us go downstairs," I said, "there are such pretty rooms there."

Then he took me in his arms and called me a blessed little goose, and said he would go down cellar if I wished, and have it whitewashed into the bargain.

But he is right enough about the beds and windows and things.

It is as airy and comfortable a room as anyone need wish, and, of course, I would not be so silly as to make him uncomfortable just for a whim.

I'm really getting quite fond of the big room, all but that horrid paper.

Out of one window I can see the garden, those mysterious deep-shaded arbors, the riotous old-fashioned flowers, and bushes and gnarly trees.

Out of another I get a lovely view of the bay and a little private wharf belonging to the estate. There is a beautiful shaded lane that runs down there from the house. I always fancy I see people walking in these numerous paths and arbors, but John has cautioned me not to give way to fancy in the least. He says that with my imaginative power and habit of story-making a nervous weakness like mine is sure to lead to all manner of excited fancies, and that I ought to use my will and good sense to check the tendency. So I try.

I think sometimes that if I were only well enough to write a little it would relieve the press of ideas and rest me.

But I find I get pretty tired when I try.

It is so discouraging not to have any advice and companionship about my work. When I get really well John says we will ask Cousin Henry and Julia down for a long visit; but he says he would as soon put fireworks in my pillow case as to let me have those stimulating people about now.

I wish I could get well faster.

But I must not think about that. This paper looks to me as if it *knew* what a vicious influence it had!

There is a recurrent spot where the pattern lolls like a broken neck and two bulbous eyes stare at you upside-down.

I get positively angry with the impertinence of it and the everlastingness. Up and down and sideways they crawl, and those absurd, unblinking eyes are everywhere. There is one place where two breadths didn't match, and the eyes go all up and down the line, one a little higher than the other.

I never saw so much expression in an inanimate thing before, and we all know how much expression they have! I used to lie awake as a child and get more entertainment and terror out of blank walls and plain furniture than most children could find in a toy store.

I remember what a kindly wink the knobs of our big old bureau used to have, and there was one chair that always seemed like a strong friend.

I used to feel that if any of the other things looked too fierce I could always hop into that chair and be safe.

The furniture in this room is no worse than inharmonious, however, for we had to bring it all from downstairs. I suppose when this was used as a playroom they had to take the nursery things out, and no wonder! I never saw such ravages as the children have made here.

The wallpaper, as I said before, is torn off in spots, and it sticketh closer than a brother—they must have had perseverance as well as hatred.

Then the floor is scratched and gouged and splintered, the plaster itself is dug out here and there, and this great heavy bed, which is all we found in the room, looks as if it had been through the wars.

But I don't mind it a bit—only the paper.

There comes John's sister. Such a dear girl as she is, and so careful of me! I must not let her find me writing.

She is a perfect, and enthusiastic housekeeper, and hopes for no better profession. I verily believe she thinks it is the writing which made me sick!

But I can write when she is out, and see her a long way off from these windows.

There is one that commands the road, a lovely, shaded, winding road, and one that just looks off over the country. A lovely country, too, full of great elms and velvet meadows.

This wallpaper has a kind of sub-pattern in a different shade, a particularly irritating one, for you can only see it in certain lights, and not clearly then.

But in the places where it isn't faded, and where the sun is just so, I can see a strange, provoking, formless sort of figure, that seems to sulk about behind that silly and conspicuous front design.

There's sister on the stairs!

Well, the Fourth of July is over! The people are gone and I am tired out. John thought it might do me good to see a little company, so we just had mother and Nellie and the children down for a week.

Of course I didn't do a thing. Jennie sees to everything now.

But it tired me all the same.

John says if I don't pick up faster he shall send me to Weir Mitchell in the fall.

But I don't want to go there at all. I had a friend who was in his hands once, and she says he is just like John and my brother, only more so!

Besides, it is such an undertaking to go so far.

I don't feel as if it was worth while to turn my hand over for anything, and I'm getting dreadfully fretful and querulous.

I cry at nothing, and cry most of the time.

Of course I don't when John is here, or anybody else, but when I am alone.

And I am alone a good deal just now. John is kept in town very often by serious cases, and Jennie is good and lets me alone when I want her to.

So I walk a little in the garden or down that lovely lane, sit on the porch under the roses, and lie down up here a good deal.

I'm getting really fond of the room in spite of the wallpaper. Perhaps *because* of the wallpaper.

It dwells in my mind so!

I lie here on this great immovable bed—it is nailed down, I believe—and follow that pattern about by the hour. It is as good as gymnastics, I assure you. I start, we'll say, at the bottom, down in the corner over there where it has not been touched, and I determine for the thousandth time that I *will* follow that pointless pattern to some sort of a conclusion.

I know a little of the principle of design, and I know this thing was not arranged on any laws of radiation, or alternation, or repetition, or symmetry, or anything else that I ever heard of.

It is repeated, of course, by the breadths, but not otherwise.

Looked at in one way each breadth stands alone, the bloated curves and flourishes—a kind of "debased Romanesque" with *delirium tremens*—go waddling up and down in isolated columns of fatuity.

But, on the other hand, they connect diagonally, and the sprawling outlines run off in great slanting waves of optic horror, like a lot of wallowing seaweeds in full chase.

The whole thing goes horizontally, too, at least it seems so, and I exhaust myself in trying to distinguish the order of its going in that direction.

They have used a horizontal breadth for a frieze, and that adds wonderfully to the confusion.

There is one end of the room where it is almost intact, and there, when the cross lights fade and the low sun shines directly upon it, I can almost fancy radiation after all—the interminable grotesques seem to form around a common centre and rush off in headlong plunges of equal distraction.

It makes me tired to follow it. I will take a nap, I guess.

I don't know why I should write this.

I don't want to.

I don't feel able.

And I know John would think it absurd. But I *must* say what I feel and think in some way—it is such a relief!

But the effort is getting to be greater than the relief.

Half the time now I am awfully lazy, and lie down ever so much.

John says I mustn't lose my strength, and has me take cod-liver oil and lots of tonics and things, to say nothing of ale and wine and rare meat.

Dear John! He loves me very dearly, and hates to have me sick. I tried to have a real earnest reasonable talk with him the other day, and tell him how I wish he would let me go and make a visit to Cousin Henry and Julia.

But he said I wasn't able to go, nor able to stand it after I got there; and I did not make out a very good case for myself, for I was crying before I had finished.

It is getting to be a great effort for me to think straight. Just this nervous weakness, I suppose.

And dear John gathered me up in his arms, and just carried me upstairs and laid me on the bed, and sat by me and read to me till it tired my head.

He said I was his darling and his comfort and all he had, and that I must take care of myself for his sake, and keep well.

He says no one but myself can help me out of it, that I must use my will and self-control and not let any silly fancies run away with me.

There's one comfort, the baby is well and happy, and does not have to occupy this nursery with the horrid wallpaper.

If we had not used it that blessed child would have! What a fortunate escape! Why, I wouldn't have a child of mine, an impressionable little thing, live in such a room for worlds.

I never thought of it before, but it is lucky that John kept me here after all. I can stand it so much easier than a baby, you see.

Of course I never mention it to them any more—I am too wise—but I keep watch of it all the same.

There are things in that paper that nobody knows but me, or ever will.

Behind that outside pattern the dim shapes get clearer every day.

It is always the same shape, only very numerous.

And it is like a woman stooping down and creeping about behind that pattern. I don't like it a bit. I wonder—I begin to think—I wish John would take me away from here!

*

It is so hard to talk with John about my case, because he is so wise, and because he loves me so.

But I tried it last night.

It was moonlight. The moon shines in all around, just as the sun does.

I hate to see it sometimes, it creeps so slowly, and always comes in by one window or another.

John was asleep and I hated to waken him, so I kept still and watched the moonlight on that undulating wallpaper till I felt creepy.

The faint figure behind seemed to shake the pattern, just as if she wanted to get out.

I got up softly and went to feel and see if the paper *did* move, and when I came back John was awake.

"What is it, little girl?" he said. "Don't go walking about like that—you'll get cold."

I though it was a good time to talk, so I told him that I really was not gaining here, and that I wished he would take me away.

"Why darling!" said he, "our lease will be up in three weeks, and I can't see how to leave before.

"The repairs are not done at home, and I cannot possibly leave town just now. Of course if you were in any danger I could and would, but you really are better, dear, whether you can see it or not. I am a doctor, dear, and I know. You are gaining flesh and color, your appetite is better. I feel really much easier about you."

"I don't weigh a bit more," said I, "nor as much; and my appetite may be better in the evening, when you are here, but it is worse in the morning when you are away."

"Bless her little heart!" said he with a big hug; "she shall be as sick as she pleases! But now let's improve the shining hours by going to sleep, and talk about it in the morning!"

"And you won't go away?" I asked gloomily.

"Why, how can I, dear? It is only three weeks more and then we will take a nice little trip of a few days while Jennie is getting the house ready. Really, dear, you are better!"

"Better in body perhaps—" I began, and stopped short, for he sat up straight and looked at me with such a stern, reproachful look that I could not say another word.

"My darling," said he, "I beg of you, for my sake and for our child's sake, as well as for your own, that you will never for one instant let that idea enter your mind! There is nothing so dangerous, so fascinating, to a temperament like yours. It is a false and foolish fancy. Can you not trust me as a physician when I tell you so?"

So of course I said no more on that score, and we went to sleep before long. He thought I was asleep first, but I wasn't—I lay there for hours trying to decide whether that front pattern and the back pattern really did move together or separately.

On a pattern like this, by daylight, there is a lack of sequence, a defiance of law, that is a constant irritant to a normal mind.

The color is hideous enough, and unreliable enough, and infuriating enough, but the pattern is torturing.

You think you have mastered it, but just as you get well under way in following, it turns a back somersault and there you are. It slaps you in the face, knocks you down, and tramples upon you. It is like a bad dream.

The outside pattern is a florid arabesque, reminding one of a fungus. If you can imagine a toadstool in joints, an interminable string of toadstools, budding and sprouting in endless convolutions—why, that is something like it.

That is, sometimes!

There is one marked peculiarity about this paper, a thing nobody seems to notice but myself, and that is that it changes as the light changes.

When the sun shoots in through the east window—I always watch for that first long, straight ray—it changes so quickly that I never can quite believe it.

That is why I watch it always.

By moonlight—the moon shines in all night when there is a moon—I wouldn't know it was the same paper.

At night in any kind of light, in twilight, candlelight, lamplight, and worst of all by moonlight, it becomes bars! The outside pattern I mean, and the woman behind it is as plain as can be.

I didn't realize for a long time what the thing was that showed behind—that dim sub-pattern—but now I am quite sure it is a woman.

By daylight she is subdued, quiet. I fancy it is the pattern that keeps her so still. It is so puzzling. It keeps me quiet by the hour.

I lie down ever so much now. John says it is good for me, and to sleep all I can.

Indeed, he started the habit by making me lie down for an hour after each meal.

It is a very bad habit, I am convinced, for, you see, I don't sleep.

And that cultivates deceit, for I don't tell them I'm awake—oh, no!

The fact is, I am getting a little afraid of John.

He seems very queer sometimes, and even Jennie has an inexplicable look.

It strikes me occasionally, just as a scientific hypothesis, that perhaps it is the paper!

I have watched John when he did not know I was looking, and come into the room suddenly on the most innocent excuses, and I've caught him several times *looking at the paper*! And Jennie too. I caught Jennie with her hand on it once.

She didn't know I was in the room, and when I asked her in a quiet, a very quiet voice, with the most restrained manner possible, what she was doing with the paper she turned around as if she had been caught stealing, and looked quite angry—asked me why I should frighten her so!

Then she said that the paper stained everything it touched, that she had found yellow smooches on all my clothes and John's, and she wished we would be more careful!

Did not that sound innocent? But I know she was studying that pattern, and I am determined that nobody shall find it out but myself!

*

Life is very much more exciting now than it used to be. You see I have something more to expect, to look forward to, to watch. I really do eat better, and am more quiet than I was.

John is so pleased to see me improve! He laughed a little the other day, and said I seemed to be flourishing in spite of my wallpaper.

I turned it off with a laugh. I had no intention of telling him it was *because* of the wallpaper—he would make fun of me. He might even want to take me away.

I don't want to leave now until I have found it out. There is a week more, and I think that will be enough.

I'm feeling ever so much better! I don't sleep much at night, for it is so interesting to watch developments; but I sleep a good deal in the daytime.

In the daytime it is tiresome and perplexing.

There are always new shoots on the fungus, and new shades of yellow all over it. I cannot keep count of them, though I have tried conscientiously.

It is the strangest yellow, that wallpaper! It makes me think of all the yellow things I ever saw—not beautiful ones like buttercups, but old foul, bad yellow things.

But there is something else about that paper—the smell! I noticed it the moment we came into the room, but with so much air and sun it was not bad. Now we have had a week of fog and rain, and whether the windows are open or not, the smell is here.

It creeps all over the house.

I find it hovering in the dining room, skulking in the parlor, hiding in the hall, lying in wait for me on the stairs.

It gets into my hair.

Even when I go to ride, if I turn my head suddenly and surprise it—there is that smell!

Such a peculiar odor, too! I have spent hours in trying to analyze it, to find what it smelled like.

It is not bad—at first, and very gentle, but quite the subtlest, most enduring odor I ever met.

In this damp weather it is awful. I wake up in the night and find it hanging over me.

It used to disturb me at first. I thought seriously of burning the house—to reach the smell.

But now I am used to it. The only thing I can think of that it is like is the *color* of the paper! A yellow smell.

There is a very funny mark on this wall, low down, near the mopboard. A streak that runs round the room. It goes behind every piece of furniture, except the bed, a long, straight, even *smooch*, as if it had been rubbed over and over.

I wonder how it was done and who did it, and what they did it for. Round and round and round—round and round and round—it makes me dizzy!

I really have discovered something at last.

Through watching so much at night, when it changes so, I have finally found out.

The front pattern *does* move—and no wonder! The woman behind shakes it!

Sometimes I think there are a great many women behind, and sometimes only one, and she crawls around fast, and her crawling shakes it all over.

Then in the very bright spots she keeps still, and in the very shady spots she just takes hold of the bars and shakes them hard.

And she is all the time trying to climb through. But nobody could climb through that pattern—it strangles so; I think that is why it has so many heads.

They get through, and then the pattern strangles them off and turns them upside-down, and makes their eyes white!

If those heads were covered or taken off it would not be half so bad.

I think that woman gets out in the daytime!

And I'll tell you why—privately—I've seen her!

I can see her out of every one of my windows!

It is the same woman, I know, for she is always creeping, and most women do not creep by daylight.

I see her on that long shaded lane, creeping up and down. I see her in those dark grape arbors, creeping all around the garden.

I see her on that long road under the trees, creeping along, and when a carriage comes she hides under the blackberry vines.

I don't blame her a bit. It must be very humiliating to be caught creeping by daylight!

I always lock the door when I creep by daylight. I can't do it at night, for I know John would suspect something at once.

And John is so queer now, that I don't want to irritate him. I wish he would take another room! Besides, I don't want anybody to get that woman out at night but myself.

I often wonder if I could see her out of all the windows at once.

But, turn as fast as I can, I can only see out of one at one time.

And though I always see her she *may* be able to creep faster than I can turn!

I have watched her sometimes away off in the open country, creeping as fast as a cloud shadow in a high wind.

If only that top pattern could be gotten off from the under one! I mean to try it, little by little.

I have found out another funny thing, but I shan't tell it this time! It does not do to trust people too much.

There are only two more days to get this paper off, and I believe John is beginning to notice. I don't like the look in his eyes.

And I heard him ask Jennie a lot of professional questions about me. She had a very good report to give.

She said I slept a good deal in the daytime.

John knows I don't sleep very well at night, for all I'm so quiet!

He asked me all sorts of questions, too, and pretended to be very loving and kind.

As if I couldn't see through him!

Still, I don't wonder he acts so, sleeping under this paper for three months.

It only interests me, but I feel sure John and Jennie are secretly affected by it.

Hurrah! This is the last day, but it is enough. John is to stay in town overnight, and won't be out until this evening.

Jennie wanted to sleep with me—the sly thing! but I told her I should undoubtedly rest better for a night all alone.

That was clever, for really I wasn't alone a bit! As soon as it was moonlight, and that poor thing began to crawl and shake the pattern, I got up and ran to help her.

I pulled and she shook, I shook and she pulled, and before morning we had peeled off yards of that paper.

A strip about as high as my head and half around the room.

And then when the sun came and that awful pattern began to laugh at me I declared I would finish it today!

We go away tomorrow, and they are moving all my furniture down again to leave things as they were before.

Jennie looked at the wall in amazement, but I told her merrily that I did it out of pure spite at the vicious thing.

She laughed and said she wouldn't mind doing it herself, but I must not get tired.

How she betrayed herself that time!

But I am here, and no person touches this paper but me—not *alive*!

She tried to get me out of the room—it was too patent! But I said it was so quiet and empty and clean now that I believed I would lie down again and sleep all I could; and not to wake me even for dinner—I would call when I woke.

So now she is gone, and the servants are gone, and the things are gone, and there is nothing left but that great bedstead nailed down, with the canvas mattress we found on it.

We shall sleep downstairs tonight, and take the boat home tomorrow.

I quite enjoy the room, now it is bare again.

How those children did tear about here!

This bedstead is fairly gnawed!

But I must get to work.

I have locked the door and thrown the key down into the front path.

I don't want to go out, and I don't want to have anybody come in, till John comes.

I want to astonish him.

I've got a rope up here that even Jennie did not find. If that woman does get out, and tries to get away, I can tie her!

But I forgot I could not reach far without anything to stand on!

This bed will *not* move!

I tried to lift and push it until I was lame, and then I got so angry I bit off a little piece at one corner—but it hurt my teeth.

Then I peeled off all the paper I could reach standing on the floor. It sticks horribly and the pattern just enjoys it! All those strangled heads and bulbous eyes and waddling fungus growths just shriek with derision!

I am getting angry enough to do something desperate. To jump out of the window would be admirable exercise, but the bars are too strong even to try.

Besides I wouldn't do it. Of course not. I know well enough that a step like that is improper and might be misconstrued.

I don't like to *look* out of the windows even—there

are so many of those creeping women, and they creep so fast.

I wonder if they all come out of that wallpaper as I did?

But I am securely fastened now by my well-hidden rope—you don't get *me* out in the road there!

I suppose I shall have to get back behind the pattern when it comes night, and that is hard!

It is so pleasant to be out in this great room and creep around as I please!

I don't want to go outside. I won't, even if Jennie asks me to.

For outside you have to creep on the ground, and everything is green instead of yellow.

But here I can creep smoothly on the floor, and my shoulder just fits in that long smooch around the wall, so I cannot lose my way.

Why, there's John at the door!

It is no use, young man, you can't open it!

How he does call and pound!

Now he's crying for an axe.

It would be a shame to break down that beautiful door!

"John dear!" said I in the gentlest voice, "the key is down by the front steps, under a plantain leaf!"

That silenced him for a few moments.

Then he said—very quietly indeed, "Open the door, my darling!"

"I can't," said I. "The key is down by the front door under a plantain leaf!"

And then I said it again, several times, very gently and slowly, and said it so often that he had to go and see, and he got it, of course, and came in. He stopped short by the door.

"What is the matter?" he cried. "For God's sake, what are you doing!"

I kept on creeping just the same, but I looked at him over my shoulder.

"I've got out at last," said I, "in spite of you and Jane! And I've pulled off most of the paper, so you can't put me back!"

Now why should that man have fainted? But he did, and right across my path by the wall, so that I had to creep over him every time!

AN ITINERANT HOUSE

Emma Frances Dawson

"Eternal longing with eternal pain,
Want without hope, and memory saddening all,
All congregated failure and despair
Shall wander there through some
old maze of wrong."

"HIS *WIFE*?" CRIED FELIPA.

"Yes," I answered, unwillingly; for until the steamer brought Mrs. Anson I believed in this Mexican woman's right to that name. I felt sorry for the bright eyes and kind heart that had cheered Anson's lodgers through weary months of early days in San Francisco.

She burst into tears. None of us knew how to comfort her. Dering spoke first:

"Beauty always wins friends." Between her sobs she repeated one of the pithy sayings of her language:

"It is as easy to find a lover as to keep a friend, but as hard to find a friend as to keep a lover."

"Yes," said Volz, "a new friendship is like a new string to your guitar—you are not sure what its tone may prove, nor how soon it may break."

"But at least its falsity is learned at once," she sobbed.

"Is it possible," I asked, "that you had no suspicion?"

"None. He told me—" She ended in a fresh gust of tears.

"The old story," muttered Dering. "Marryatt's skipper was right in thinking everything that once happened would come again somewhere."

Anson came. He had left the newcomer at the Niantic, on pretense of putting his house in order. Felipa turned on him before we could go.

"Is this true?" she cried.

Without reply he went to the window and stood looking out. She sprang toward him, with rage distorting her face.

"Coward!" she screamed, in fierce scorn.

Then she fell senseless. Two doctors were called. One said she was dead. The other, at first doubtful, vainly tried hot sealing wax and other tests. After thirty-six hours her funeral was planned. Yet Dering, once medical student, had seen an electric current used in such a case in Vienna, and wanted to try it. That night, he, Volz, and I offered to watch. When all was still, Dering, who had smuggled in the simple things needed, began his weird work.

"Is it not too late?" I asked.

"Every corpse," said he, "can be thus excited soon after death, for a brief time only, and but once. If the body is not lifeless, the electric current has power at any time."

Volz, too nervous to stay near, stood in the door open to the dark hall. It was a dreadful sight. The dead woman's breast rose and fell; smiles and frowns flitted across her face.

"The body begins to react finely," cried Dering, making Volz open the windows, while I wrapped hot blankets round Felipa, and he instilled clear coffee and brandy.

"It seems like sacrilege! Let her alone!" I exclaimed. "Better dead than alive!"

"My God! say not that!" cried Volz; "the nerve which hears is last to die. She may know all we say."

"Musical bosh!" I muttered.

"Perhaps not," said Dering; "in magnetic sleep that nerve can be roused."

The night seemed endless. The room gained an uncanny look, the macaws on the gaudy, old-fashioned wallpaper seemed fluttering and changing places. Volz crouched in a heap near the door. Dering stood by Felipa, watching closely. I paced the shadowy room, looked at the gleam of the moon on the bay, listened to the soughing wind in the gum trees mocking the sea, and tried to recall more cheerful scenes, but always bent under the weight of that fearful test going on beside me. Where was her soul? Beyond the stars, in the room with us, or "like trodden snowdrift melting in the dark"? Volz came behind, startling me by grasping my elbow.

"Shall I not play?" he whispered. "Familiar music is remembrance changed to sound—it brings the past as perfume does. Gypsy music in her ear would be like holding wild flowers to her nostrils."

"Ask Dering," I said; "he will know best."

I heard him urging Dering.

"She has gypsy blood," he said; "their music will rouse her." Dering unwillingly agreed. "But nothing abrupt—begin low," said he.

Vaguely uneasy, I turned to object; but Volz had gone for his violin. Far off arose a soft, wavering, sleepy strain, like a wind blowing over a field of poppies. He passed, in slow, dramatic style, through the hall, playing on the way. As he came in, oddly sustained notes trembled like sighs and sobs; these were by degrees subdued, though with spasmodic outbursts, amid a grand movement as of phantom shapes through cloud-land. One heart-rending phrase recurring as of one of the shadowy host striving to break loose, but beaten back by impalpable throngs, numberless grace notes trailing their sparks like fireworks. No music of our intervals and our rhythms, but perplexing in its charm like a draught that maddens. Time, space, our very identities, were consumed in this white heat of sound. I held my breath. I caught his arm.

"It is too bold and distracting," I cried. "It is enough to kill us! Do you expect to torment her back? How can it affect us so?"

"Because," he answered, laying down his violin and wiping his brow, "in the gypsy minor scale the fourth and seventh are augmented. The sixth is diminished. The frequent augmentation of the fourth makes that sense of unrest."

"Bah! Technical terms make it no plainer," I said, returning to the window.

He played a whispered, merry discordance, resolving into click of castanets, laugh, and dance of a gypsy camp. Out of the whirl of flying steps and tremolo of tambourines rose a tender voice, asking, denying, sighing, imploring, passing into an overruling, long-drawn call that vibrated in widening rings to reach the farthest horizon—nay, beyond land or sea, "east of the sun, west of the moon." With a rush returned the wild jollity of men's bass laughter, women's shrill reply, the stir of the gypsy camp. This dropped behind vague, rolling measures of clouds and chaos, where to and fro floated grotesque goblins of grace notes like the fancies of a madman; struggling, rising, falling, vain-reaching strains; fierce cries like commands. The music seemed another vital essence thrilling us with its own emotion.

"No more, no more!" I cried, half gasping, and grasping Volz's arm. "What is it, Dering?"

He had staggered from the bed and was trying to see his watch. "It is just forty-four hours!" he said, pointing to Felipa.

Her eyes were open! We were alarmed as if doing wrong and silently watched her. Fifteen minutes later her lips formed one word:

"Idiots!"

Half an hour after she flung the violin from bed to floor, but would not speak. People began to stir about the house. The prosaic sounds jarred on our strained nerves. We felt brought from another sphere. Volz and I were going, but Felipa's upraised hand kept us. She sat up, looking a ghastly vision. Turning first toward me she quoted my words:

"'Better dead than alive!' True. You knew I would be glad to die. What right had you to bring me back? God's curses on you! I was dead. Then came agony. I heard your voices. I thought we were all in hell. Then I found how by your evil cunning I was to be forced to live. It was like an awful nightmare. I shall not forget you, nor you me. These very walls shall remember—here, where I have been so tortured no one shall have peace! Fools! Leave me! Never come in this room again!"

We went, all talking at once, Dering angry at her mood; Volz, sorry he had not reached a soothing *pianissimo* passage; I, owning we had no right to make the test. We saw her but once more, when with a threatening nod toward us she left the house.

From that time a gloom settled over the place. Mrs. Anson proved a hard-faced, cold-hearted, Cape Cod woman, a scold and drudge, who hated us as much as we disliked her. Homesick and unhappy, she soon went East and died. Within a year, Anson was found dead where he had gone hunting in the Saucelito woods, supposed a suicide; Dering was hung by the Vigilantes, and the rest were scattered on the four winds. Volz and I were last to go. The night before we sailed, he for Australia, I for New York, he said:

"I am sorry for those who come after us in this house."

"Not knowing of any tragedy here," I said, "they will not feel its influence."

"They must feel it," he insisted; "it is written in the Proverbs, 'Evil shall not depart from his house.'"

Some years later, I was among passengers embarking at New York for California, when there was a cry of "Man overboard!" In the confusion of his rescue, among heartless and pitiful talk, I overheard one man declare that the drowned might be revived.

"Oh, yes!" cried a well-known voice behind me. "But they might not thank you."

I turned—to find Volz! He was coming out with Wynne, the actor. Enjoying our comradeship on the voyage, on reaching San Francisco we took rooms together, on Bush Street, in an old house with a large garden. Volz became leader of the orchestra, and Wynne, leading man at the same theatre. Lest my folks, a Maine deacon's family, should think I was on the road to ruin, I told in letters home only of the city missionary in the house.

Volz was hard worked. Wynne was not much liked. My business went wrong. It rained for many weeks; to this we laid the discomfort that grew to weigh on us. Volz wreaked his sense of it on his violin, adding to the torment of Wynne and myself, for to lonesome anxious souls "the demon in music" shows horns and cloven foot in the trying sounds of practice. One Sunday Volz played the 'Witches Dance,' the 'Dream,' and 'The Long, Long Weary Day.'

"I can bear it no longer!" said Wynne. "I feel like the haunted Matthias in *The Bells*. If I could feel so when acting such parts, it would make my fortune. But I feel it only here."

"I think," said Volz, "it is the *gloria fonda* bush near the window; the scent is too strong." He dashed off Strauss's fretful, conflicting 'Hurry and Delay.'

"There, there! It is too much," said I. "You express my feelings."

He looked doubtful. "Put it in words," said he.

"How can I?" I said. "When our firm sent me abroad, I went sightseeing among old palaces, whose Gobelin tapestries framed in their walls were faded to gray phantoms of pictures, but out of some the thrilling eyes followed me till I could not stay in their range. My feeling here is the uneasy one of being watched."

"Ha!" said Volz. "You remind me of Heine, when he wrote from Livorno. He knew no Italian, but the old palaces whispered secrets unheard by day. The moon was interpreter, knew the lapidary style, translated to dialect of his heart."

"Strange effects after the moon," mused Wynne. "That gives new meaning to Kent's threat: 'I'll make a sop o' the moonshine of you!'"

Volz went on: "Heine wrote: 'The stones here speak to me, and I know their mute language. Also, they seem deeply to feel what I think. So a broken column of the old Roman times, an old tower of Lombardy, a weather-beaten Gothic piece of a pillar understands me well. But I am a ruin myself, wandering among ruins.'"

"Perhaps, like Poe's hero," said I, "'I have imbibed shadows of fallen columns at Balbec, and Tadmor, and Persepolis, until my very soul has become a ruin.'"

"But I, too," said Wynne, "feel the unrest of Tannhäuser:

'Alas! what seek I here, or anywhere,
Whose way of life is like the crumbled stair
That winds and winds about a ruined tower,
And leads no whither.'"

"I am oppressed," Volz owned, "as if someone in my presence was suffering deeply."

"I feel," said Wynne, "as if the scene was not set right for the performance now going on. There is a hitch and drag somewhere—scene-shifters on a strike. Happy are you poets and musicians, who can express what is vague."

Volz laughed. "As in Liszt's oratorio of *Christus*," said he, "where a sharp, ear-piercing *sostenuto* on the piccolo flute shows the shining of the star of Bethlehem." He turned to me. "Schubert's 'Wanderer' always recalls to me a house you and I know to be under a ban."

"Haunted?" asked Wynne. "Of all speculative theories, St. Martin's sends the most cold thrills up one's back. He said none of the dead come back, but some stay."

"What we Germans call *gebannt*—tied to one spot," said Volz. "But this is no ghost, only a proof of what a German psychologist holds, that the magnetic man is a spirit."

"Go on, 'and tell quaint lies'—I like them," said Wynne.

I told in brief outline, with no names, the tale Volz and I knew, while we strolled to Telegraph Hill, passing five streets blocked by the roving houses common to San Francisco.

Wynne said: "They seem to have minds of their own, with their entrances and exits in a *moving* drama."

"Sort of 'Poor Jo's,'" said I.

"Castles in chess," said Volz.

"Io-like," said Wynne, "with a gad in their hearts that forever drives them on."

A few foreign sailors lounged on the hilltop, looking at the view. The wind blew such a gale we did not stay. The steps we had known, cut in the side, were gone. Where the old house used to be, goats were browsing.

"Perchance we do inhabit it but now," mockingly cried Wynne; "methinks it must be so."

"Then," said Volz, thoughtfully, "it might be what Germans call 'far-working'—acted in distance—that affects us."

"What do you mean?" I asked. "Do you know anything of her now?"

"I know she went to Mexico," said he; "that is all."

"What is 'far-working'?" asked Wynne. "If I could act in the distance, and here too—'what larks!'"

"Yes—'if,'" said I. "Think how all our lives turn on that pivot. Suppose Hawthorne's offer to join Wilkes's exploring expedition had been taken!"

"Only to wills that know no 'if' is 'far-working' possible," said Volz. "Substance or space can no more hinder this force than the one of mineral magnetism. Passavent joins it with pictures falling, or watches stopping at the time of a death. In sleep-walking, some kinds of illness, or nearness of death, the nervous ether is not so closely allied to its material conductors, the nerves, and may be loosened to act from afar, the surest where blood or feeling makes attraction or repulsion."

Wynne in the two voices of the play repeated:

"VICTOR.—Where is the gentleman?
CHISPE.—As the old song says:
'His body is in Segovia,
His soul is in Madrid.'"

We could learn about the house we were in only that five families had moved in and out during the last year. Wynne resolved to shake off the gloom that wrapped us. In struggles to defy it, he on the strength of a thousand-dollar benefit, made one payment on the house and began repairs.

On an off-night he was vainly trying to study a new part. Volz advised the relief to his nerves of reciting the dream scene from *The Bells*, reminding him he had compared it with his restlessness there. Wynne denied it.

"Yes," said Volz, "where the mesmerizer forces Matthias to confess."

But Wynne refused, as if vexed, till Volz offered to show in music his own mood, and I agreed to read some rhymes about mine. Volz was long tuning his violin.

"I feel," he said, "as if the passers-by would hear a secret. Music is such a subtle expression of emotion—like flower odor rolls far and affects the stranger. Hearken! In Heine's *Reisebilder*, as the cross was thrown ringing on the banquet table of the gods, they grew dumb and pale, and even paler till they melted in mist. So shall you at the long-drawn wail of my violin grow breathless, and fade from each other's sight."

The music closed round us, and we waited in its deep solitude. One brief, sad phrase fell from airy heights to lowest depths into a sea of sound, whose harmonious eddies as they widened breathed of passion and pain, now swooning, now reviving, with odd pauses and sighs that rose to cries of despair, but the tormenting first strain recurring fainter and fainter, as if drowning, drowning, drowned—yet floating back for repeated last plaint, as if not to be quelled, and closing, as it began, the whole.

As I read the name of my verses, Volz murmured: "*Les Nuits Blanches*. No. 4. Stephen Heller."

SLEEPLESS NIGHTS.

Against the garden's mossy paling
  I lean, and wish the night away,
Whose faint, unequal shadows trailing
  Seem but a dream of those of day.

Sleep burdens blossom, bud, and leaf,
  My soul alone aspires, dilates,
Yearns to forget its care and grief—
  No bath of sleep its pain abates.

How dread these dreams of wide-eyed nights!
  What is, and is not, both I rue,
My wild thoughts fly like wand'ring kites,
  No peace falls with this balmy dew.

Through slumb'rous stillness, scarcely stirred
By sudden trembles, as when shifts
O'er placid pool some skimming bird,
Its Lethean bowl a poppy lifts.

If one deep draught my doubts could solve,
The world might bubble down its brim,
Like Cleopatra's pearl dissolve,
With all my dreams within its rim.

What should I know but calm repose?
How feel, recalling this lost sphere?
Alas! the fabled poppy shows
Upon its bleeding heart—a tear!

Wynne unwillingly began to recite: "'I fear nothing, but dreams are dreams—'"

He stammered, could not go on, and fell to the floor. We got him to bed. He never spoke sanely after. His wild fancies appalled us watching him all night.

"Avaunt Sathanas! That's not my cue," he muttered. "A full house tonight. How could Talma forget how the crowd looked, and fancy it a pack of skeletons? Tell Volz to keep the violins playing through this scene, it works me up as well as thrills the audience. Oh, what tiresome nights I have lately, always dreaming of scenes where rival women move, as in *Court and Stage*, where, all masked, the king makes love to Frances Stewart before the queen's face! How do I try to cure it? 'And being thus frighted, swear a prayer or two and sleep again.' Madame, you're late; you've too little rouge; you'll look ghastly. We're not called yet; let's rehearse our scene. Now, then, I enter left, pass to the window. You cry 'is this true?' and faint. All crowd about. Quick curtain."

Volz and I looked at each other.

"Can our magnetism make his senses so sharp that he knows what is in our minds?" he asked me.

"Nonsense!" I said. "Memory, laudanum, and whisky."

"There," Wynne went on, "the orchestra is stopping. They've rung up the curtain. Don't hold me. The stage waits, yet how can I go outside my door to step on dead bodies? Street and sidewalk are knee-deep with them. They rise and curse me for disturbing them. I lift my cane to strike. It turns to a snake, whose slimy body writhes in my hand. Trying to hold it from biting me, my nails cut my palm till blood streams to drown the snake."

He awed us not alone from having no control of his thoughts, but because there came now and then a strange influx of emotion as if other souls passed in and out of his body.

"Is this hell?" he groaned. "What blank darkness! Where am I? What is that infernal music haunting me through all space? If I could only escape it I need not go back to earth—to that room where I feel choked, where the very wallpaper frets me with its flaunting birds flying to and fro, mocking my fettered state. 'Here, here in the very den of the wolf!' Hallo, Benvolio, call boy's hunting you. Romeo's gone on.

'See where he steals—
Locked in some gloomy covert under key
Of cautionary silence, with his arms
Threaded, like these cross-boughs, in sorrow's knot.'

What is this dread that weighs like a nightmare? 'I do not fear; like Macbeth, I only inhabit trembling.' 'For one of them—she is in hell already, and burns, poor soul! For the other'—Ah! must I die here, alone in the woods, felled by a coward, Indian-like, from behind a tree? None of the boys will know. 'I just now come from a whole world of mad women that had almost—what, is she dead?' Poor Felipa!"

"Did you tell him her name?" I asked Volz.

"No," said he. "Can one man's madness be another's real life?"

"Blood was spilt—the avenger's wing hovered above my house," raved Wynne. "What are these lights, hundreds of them—serpent's eyes? Is it the audience—coiled, many-headed monster, following me round the world? Why do they hiss? I've played this part a hundred times. 'Taught by Rage, and Hunger, and Despair?' Do they, full-fed, well-clothed, light-hearted, know how to judge me? 'A plague on both your houses!' What is that flame? Fire that consumes my vitals—spon-ta-neous combustion! It is then possible. Water! water!"

The doctor said there had been some great strain on Wynne's mind. He sank fast, though we did all we could. Toward morning I turned to Volz with the words:

"He is dead."

The city missionary was passing the open door. He grimly muttered:

"Better dead than alive!"

"My God! say not that!" cried Volz. "The nerve which hears is last to die. He may know—"

He faltered. We stood aghast. The room grew suddenly familiar. I tore off a strip of the gray tint on the walls. Under it we found the old paper with its bright macaws.

"Ah, ha!" Volz said; "will you now deny my theory of 'far-working'?"

Dazed, I could barely murmur: "Then people can be affected by it!"

"Certainly," said he, "as rubbed glasses gain electric power."

Within a week we sailed—he for Brazil, I for New York.

Several years after, at Sacramento, Arne, an artist I had known abroad, found me on the overland train, and on reaching San Francisco urged me to go where he lodged.

"I am low-spirited here," he said; "I don't know why."

I stopped short on the crowded wharf. "Where do you live?" I asked.

"Far up Market Street," said he.

"What sort of a house?" I insisted.

"Oh—nothing modern—over a store," he answered. Reassured, I went with him. He lived in a jumble of easels, portfolios, paint, canvas, bits of statuary, casts, carvings, foils, red curtains, Chinese goatskins, woodcuts, photographs, sketches, and unfinished pictures. On the wall hung a scene from *The Wandering Jew*, as we saw it at the Adelphi, in London, where in the Arctic regions he sees visions foreshadowing the future of his race. Under it was quoted:

——"All in my mind is confused, nor can I dissever
The mould of the visible world from the shape of
  my thought in me—
The Inward and Outward are fused, and through
  them murmur forever
The sorrow whose sound is the wind and the roar
  of the limitless sea."

"Do you remember," Arne asked, "when we saw that play? Both younger and more hopeful. How has the world used you? As for me, I have done nothing since I came here but that sketch, finished months ago. I have not lost ambition, but I feel fettered."

"Absinthe?—opium?—tobacco?" I hinted.

"Neither," he answered. "I try to work, but visions, widely different from what I will, crowd on me, as on the Jew in the play. Not the unconscious brain action all thinkers know, but a dictation from without. No rush of creative impulses, but a dragging sense of something else I ought to paint."

"Briefly," I said, "you are a 'Haunted Man.'"

"Haunted by a willful design," said he. "I feel as if something had happened somewhere which I *must* show."

"What is it like?" I asked.

"I wish I could tell you," he replied. "But only odd bits change places, like looking in a kaleidoscope; yet all cluster around one centre."

One day, looking over his portfolios, I found an old *Temple Bar*, which he said he kept for this passage—which he read to me—from T.A. Trollope's 'Artist's Tragedy':

> "The old walls and ceilings and floors must be saturated with the exhalations of human emotions! These lintels, doorways, and stairs have become, by long use and homeliness, dear to human hearts, and have become so intimately blended a portion of the mental furniture of human lives, that they have contributed their part to the formation of human characters. Such facts and considerations have gone to the fashioning of the mental habitudes of all of us. If all could have been recorded! If emotion had the property of photographing itself on the surfaces of the walls which had witnessed it! Even if only passion, when translated into acts, could have done so! Ah, what palimpsests! What deciphering of

tangled records! What skillful separation of successive layers of 'passionography'!"

"I know a room," said Arne, "thronged with acts that elbow me from my work and fill me with unrest."

I looked at him in mute surprise.

"I suppose," he went on, "such things do not interest you."

"No—yes," I stammered. "I have marked in traveling how lonely houses change their expression as you come near, pass, and leave them. Some frown, others smile. The Bible buildings had life of their own and human diseases; the priests cursed or blessed them as men."

"Houses seem to remember," said he. "Some rooms oppress us with a sense of lives that have been lived in them."

"That," I said, "is like Draper's theory of shadows on walls always staying. He shows how after a breath passes over a coin or key, its spectral outline remains for months after the substance is removed. But can the mist of circumstance sweeping over us make our vacant places hold any trace of us?"

"Why not? Who can deny it? Why do you look at me so?" he asked.

I could not tell him the sad tale. I hesitated; then said: "I was thinking of Volz, a friend I had, who not only believed in what Bulwer calls 'a power akin to mesmerism and superior to it, once called Magic, and that it might reach over the dead, so far as their experience on earth,' but also in animal magnetism from any distance."

Arne grew queerly excited. "If Time and Space exist but in our thoughts, why should it not be true?" said he. "Macdonald's lover cries, 'That which has been is, and the Past can never cease. She is mine, and I shall find her—what matters it when, or where, or how?'" He sighed. "In Acapulco, a year ago, I saw a woman who has been before me ever since—the centre of the circling, changing, crude fancies that trouble me."

"Did you know her?" I asked.

"No, nor anything about her, not even her name. It is like a spell. I must paint her before anything else, but I cannot yet decide how. I feel sure she has played a tragic part in some life-drama."

"Swinburne's queen of panthers," I hinted.

"Yes. But I was not in love. Love I must forgo. I am not a man with an income."

"I know you are not a nincompoop!" I said, always

trying to change such themes by a jest. I could not tell him I knew a place which had the influence he talked of. I could not revisit that house.

Soon after he told me he had begun his picture, but would not show it. He complained that one figure kept its back toward him. He worked on it till he fell ill. Even then he hid it. "Only a layer of passionography," he said.

I grew restless. I thought his mood affected mine. It was a torment as well as a puzzle to me that his whole talk should be of the influence of houses, rooms, even personal property that had known other owners. Once I asked him if he had anything like the brown coat Sheridan swore drew ill-luck to him.

"Sometimes I think," he answered, "it is this special brown paint artists prize which affects me. It is made from the best asphaltum, and that can be got only from Egyptian mummy cloths. Very likely dust of the mummies is ground in it. I ought to feel their ill-will."

One day I went to Saucelito. In the still woods I forgot my unrest till coming to the stream where, as I suddenly remembered, Anson was found dead, a dread took me which I tried to lose by putting into rhyme. Turning my pockets at night, I crumpled the page I had written on, and threw it on the floor.

In uneasy sleep I dreamed I was again in Paris, not where I liked to recall being, but at "Bullier's," and in wartime. The bald, spectacled leader of the orchestra, leaning back, shamming sleep, while a dancing, stamping, screaming crowd wave tri-colored flags, and call for the 'Chant du départ.' Three thousand voices in a rushing roar that makes the twenty thousand lights waver, in spasmodic but steady chorus:

"*Les departs—parts—parts!*
Les departs—parts—parts!
Les departs—parts—parts!"

Roused, I supposed by passing rioters, I did not try to sleep again, but rose to write a letter for the early mail. As I struck a light I saw, smoothed out on the table, the wrinkled page I had cast aside. The ink was yet wet on two lines added to each verse. A chill crept over me as I read:

FOREST MURMURS.

Across the woodland bridge I pass,
  And sway its three long, narrow planks,
To mark how gliding waters glass
  Bright blossoms doubled ranks on ranks;
And how through tangle of the ferns

Floats incense from veiled flower urns,
What would the babbling brook reveal?
What may these trembling depths conceal?
Dread secret of the dense woods, held
With restless shudders horror-spelled!

How shift the shadows of the wood,
  As if it tossed in troubled sleep!
Strange whispers, vaguely understood,
  Above, below, around me creep;
While in the sombre-shadowed stream
Great scarlet splashes far down gleam,
The odd-reflected, stately shapes
Of cardinals in crimson capes;
Not those—but spectral pools of blood
That stain these sands through strongest flood!

Like blare of trumpets through black nights—
  Or sunset clouds before a storm—
Are these red phantom water-sprites
  That mock me with fantastic form;
With flitting of the last year's bird Fled ripples
that its low flight stirred—
How should these rushing waters learn
Aught but the bend of this year's fern?
The lonesome wood, with bated breath,
Hints of a hidden blow—and death!

I could not stay alone. I ran to Arne's room. As I knocked, the falling of some light thing within made me think he was stirring. I went in. He sat in the moonlight, back to me before his easel. The picture on it might be the one he kept secret. I would not look. I went to his side and touched him. He had been dead for hours! I turned the unseen canvas to the wall.

Next day I packed and planned to go east. I paid the landlady not to send Arne's body to the morgue, and watched it that night, when a sudden memory swept over me like a tidal wave. There was a likeness in the room to one where I had before watched the dead. Yes—there were the windows, there the doors—just here stood the bed, in the same spot I sat. What wildness was in the air of San Francisco!

To put such crazy thoughts to flight I would look at Arne's last work. Yet I wavered, and more than once turned away after laying my hand on it. At last I snatched it, placed it on the easel and lighted the nearest gas-burner before looking at it. Then—great heavens! How had this vision come to Arne? It was the scene where Felipa cursed us. Every detail of the room reproduced, even the gay birds on the wallpaper, and her flowerpots. The figures and faces of

Dering and Volz were true as hers, and in the figure with averted face which Arne had said kept its back to him, I knew—myself! What strange insight had he gained by looking at Felipa? It was like the man who trembled before the unknown portrait of the Marquise de Brinvilliers.

How long I gazed at the picture I do not know. I heard, without heeding, the doorbell ring and steps along the hall. Voices. Someone looking at rooms. The landlady, saying this room was to let, but unwilling to show it, forced to own its last tenant lay there dead. This seemed no shock to the stranger.

"Well," said her shrill tones, "poor as he was he's better dead than alive!"

The door opened as a well-known voice cried: "My God! say not that! The nerve which hears is last to die—"

Volz stood before me! Awe-struck, we looked at each other in silence. Then he waved his hand to and fro before his eyes.

"Is this a dream?" he said. "There," pointing to the bed; "you"—to me; "the same words—the very room! Is it our fate?"

I pointed to the picture and to Arne. "The last work of this man, who thought it a fancy sketch?"

While Volz stood dumb and motionless before it, the landlady spoke:

"Then you know the place. Can you tell what ails it? There have been suicides in this room. No one prospers in the house. My cousin, who is a house-mover, warned me against taking it. He says before the store was put under it here it stood on Bush Street, and before that on Telegraph Hill."

Volz clutched my arm. "It is *The Flying Dutchman* of a house!" he cried, and drew me fast downstairs and out into a dense fog which made the world seem a tale that was told, blotting out all but our two slanting forms, bent as by what poor Wynne would have called "a blast from hell," hurrying blindly away. I heard the voice of Volz as if from afar: "The magnetic man *is* a spirit!"

Pushkin Press

Pushkin Press was founded in 1997, and publishes novels, essays, memoirs, children's books—everything from timeless classics to the urgent and contemporary.

This book is part of the Pushkin Collection of paperbacks, designed to be as satisfying as possible to hold and to enjoy. It is typeset in Monotype Baskerville, based on the transitional English serif typeface designed in the mid-eighteenth century by John Baskerville. It was litho-printed on Munken Premium White Paper and notch-bound by the independently owned printer TJ International in Padstow, Cornwall. The cover, with French flaps, was printed on Rives Linear Bright White paper. The paper and cover board are both acid-free and Forest Stewardship Council (FSC) certified.

Pushkin Press publishes the best writing from around the world—great stories, beautifully produced, to be read and read again.

STEFAN ZWEIG · EDGAR ALLAN POE · ISAAC BABEL
TOMÁS GONZÁLEZ · ULRICH PLENZDORF · JOSEPH KESSEL
VELIBOR ČOLIĆ · LOUISE DE VILMORIN · MARCEL AYMÉ
ALEXANDER PUSHKIN · MAXIM BILLER · JULIEN GRACQ
BROTHERS GRIMM · HUGO VON HOFMANNSTHAL
GEORGE SAND · PHILIPPE BEAUSSANT · IVÁN REPILA
E.T.A. HOFFMANN · ALEXANDER LERNET-HOLENIA
YASUSHI INOUE · HENRY JAMES · FRIEDRICH TORBERG
ARTHUR SCHNITZLER · ANTOINE DE SAINT-EXUPÉRY
MACHI TAWARA · GAITO GAZDANOV · HERMANN HESSE
LOUIS COUPERUS · JAN JACOB SLAUERHOFF
PAUL MORAND · MARK TWAIN · PAUL FOURNEL
ANTAL SZERB · JONA OBERSKI · MEDARDO FRAILE
HÉCTOR ABAD · PETER HANDKE · ERNST WEISS
PENELOPE DELTA · RAYMOND RADIGUET · PETR KRÁL
ITALO SVEVO · RÉGIS DEBRAY · BRUNO SCHULZ · TEFFI
EGON HOSTOVSKÝ · JOHANNES URZIDIL · JÓZEF WITTLIN